We were both drenched by the end of the forty-five minute workout. "Be sure to drink a lot of water while you're here. The humidity just soaks it out of you and dehydration can level you in less than a day."

"Thanks." She slung a towel around her neck, and it framed her collarbone. We stared at each other and I felt next to naked. When I picked up my Bosu ball to stow in the large locker, she followed suit.

I leaned into the locker to get the ball into the best position so the door would close. The locker had been large enough for mats and barbells, but the Bosu balls were stressing its limits.

A wave of tingling goosepimples swept over me as Celine leaned in too, her body the length of mine. In my ear she said, "Here's the other one."

I shuddered. Her pelvis rocked against my ass. Part of me couldn't believe this was happening—Celine Griffin!—while the rest of me had stopped thinking at all. I choked back a moan but couldn't stop my hips from moving in response to her.

The open door sheltered us temporarily and Celine had no doubt noticed that. Again, her low voice melted into my ear. "I think I'm not the only one who'd like a massage."

ALL THE WRONG PLACES

BY

KARIN KALLMAKER

Bella
BOOKS

2004

Copyright© 2004 by Karin Kallmaker

Bella Books, Inc.
P.O. Box 10543
Tallahassee, FL 32302

Printed in the United States of America on acid-free paper
First Edition

Editor: Christi Cassidy
Cover designer: Bonnie Liss (Phoenix Graphics)

ISBN 1-931513-76-7

For Maria,

who taught, learned and grew so we could be bad

Sweet Fifteen, and ready to grow up

Chapter One

"Now lace your fingers behind your left calf and stretch those toes toward the crown of your head." I kept my tone in the blended range between soothing and energized. Experience had taught me one could be too perky at nine a.m. for people on vacation.

There were nearly twenty for Morning Stretch, a good turnout for a Saturday morning. Most would be heading home in a few hours after their week of Florida sun, food and activities, but one last stretch in the cool, early-morning air was a popular event. For many it was a last chance to enjoy the shadiest portion of the private Sanibel Island beach while it was still quiet.

"Now the other side, and count slowly to ten." I felt a twinge in my knee and eased up on the pressure. A glance at the participants told me most were following form. Tomorrow it would be nothing but first-timers, but that was part of the fun of my job. There were always new faces.

Through my lashes I watched the palm fronds overhead move easily in the light breeze. The sky was an endless pale blue this morning and the sun had not yet risen over the resort buildings. It was cool and peaceful. The only other time of day I liked more was first light on a golf course.

A minor commotion made me look up again and I quickly hid a smile. The late arrival was Paige, a woman I had been exchanging glances with since her arrival last Saturday. Paige— oh no, or was it Penny, penny for your thoughts? Paige, like a book, I recalled. When you meet as many new people as I do, mnemonics are useful. It was a trick I'd learned from my father, and one of the few things of his for which I had any use at all.

Paige, like a book, had no trouble with the inner thigh stretches, and I seriously doubted she was unaware that her mat was turned so I could see just how flexible her legs were. Bronzed, fit, generously curved with thick curls of sandy blonde hair—Paige was my type. But then, as my best friend Tess would say, all women seem to be my type.

Paige really only had one drawback as a potential playmate, and that was the boyfriend with whom she had arrived. Scuttlebutt was he'd proposed two nights ago, but there was no sign of a ring and he hadn't seemed all that happy when I'd caught a glimpse of him slamming serves on the tennis court.

"Take your left elbow in your right hand and stretch, gently, over your head. That's it! Just think how many of these exercises you can do sitting at your desk at work."

"Sure, Brandy." The woman nearest to me, whose name I'd never picked up, was always good for a wisecrack. "Like I'll remember how to put my left heel over my right shoulder while I press down through my inner left hip and relax my right pinky."

I chuckled. "It's not that bad. Whatever feels good you'll remember. It's time to breathe and relax. Knowing how to truly relax is very important to our well-being. Let's all stretch out on our mats."

For a minute there was only the sound of surf on the sand. I fought a yawn. I hadn't been up that late but morning had still seemed to arrive early for a Saturday in April.

Paige, like a book, was the last to rise from her mat when I called a close to the class. The white swimsuit she wore was barely covered by a crimson beach coverup. She smiled at me, her eyebrows making suggestions as they had all week, then she turned to pick up her mat. The view was very nice, very nice indeed. It was a real pity about the boyfriend.

"Who's joining me for Body Pump?" Tess, looking as bright and cheerful as the light sparkling across the offshore white-caps, gestured in the direction of Club Sandzibel's fitness center.

I don't know how she managed to look so wide awake when she'd probably closed the bar the night before. She'd told me that the new bartender, Jean-Paul, seemed fun, and there was no reason to think she hadn't explored some possibilities with him.

"Hey, Brandy," she said to me as she bounced happily on the balls of her feet. "I need to show you the new Bosu lunges. Better for inner thigh work and easier for first-timers."

"I'll be along in just a bit then." I checked the area to ensure the mats were back in their covered storage container and that all the guests seemed content. Of course, this meant I eventually had to make eye contact with Paige.

"Must you go so soon?" She spoke with a soft drawl that was musical but not cloying.

"You'll be going soon, for good." I waved at Tess, who gave me a knowing wink as she left. I watched her blonde ponytail sway against her back, then turned back to Paige.

"I've had a wonderful week. There are plenty of reasons to come back here. The setting, the great food . . . the wonderful staff." With that she gave me the same, almost involuntary once-over that had sent a wicked jolt down my spine last Saturday, when she had arrived.

I'd been working at Club Sandzibel for two years, and it was Tess who had first told me that some of the guests presumed the staff were available for private romping, and that was why they chose a resort oriented toward younger, more active guests and staffed with younger, more active personnel. Management denied any pressure at all, and there was even training on how to graciously refuse an overture. But higher-ups also clearly said that activities carried out while we were off duty were not of concern unless other guests were made in any way uncomfortable by them.

I wondered how uncomfortable Paige's boyfriend would be if Paige and I hopped back to my quarters for an hour. The idea had appeal, though I wasn't sure why. When I'd first started working at the resort I'd been like a dyke at a softball game. So many women, so little time. But the allure of straight-but-looking-for-thrills Paiges had paled along the way.

I gave Paige a long look, though. The fact that she was in the mood and so was I made analyzing whys and wherefores less important at the moment. Something about her appealed. She had sought me out and as far as I was concerned, her actions and conscience were her own business. But, I remembered, time was short and I had places I needed to be.

"Is there someplace we could talk for a few minutes? I know you have to go to the next class."

"Why don't you walk over to Body Pump with me?" If she wanted to make some sort of confused declaration then I could make time to listen. But there wasn't time for anything else, at least, not the way I liked to do it.

A walk wasn't what she had in mind, but she fell into step and I caught the complicated scent of a lilac blend that I'd noticed before around her. She was perhaps four inches taller than me, but then so is most of the world when you're five-two.

During the walk to Adult Fitness I changed my mind. Maybe it was because she was leaving. Maybe it was because from the moment she'd arrived she'd looked at me like I could teach her more than aerobics and stretching. Maybe it was because she smelled good and it was still early on a glorious spring morning. What was it Tess had said on my birthday? That when she'd been twenty-six she wished she'd noticed the mornings more. At nearly thirty-two, Tess claimed time was already making her hate first light—that is, when she was lucid enough to see it.

Paige followed me past the gathering of Bosu ball devotees and into the gym. The TV at one end was blaring CNN talking heads while the opposite monitor was competing with equally loud MTV. Clanging weight machines added to the cacophony. I stopped for a sip of water to fight down a nervous flutter. My throat was suddenly dry. My crotch was not.

I think if she hadn't looked a little bit vulnerable, like she really didn't do this sort of thing all the time, I might have turned back to Tess's class. But Paige seemed hesitant, as if she'd gotten this far on bravado and a good flirtatious line, not practice.

"We can get some more towels from the supply room." I led the way.

"Staff only," she read on the sign.

"We make the occasional exception." My tone was not as light as I had hoped. I swiped my pass card with all the nonchalance I could muster and opened the door for her.

It was her choice then. She knew at a minimum we would do some heavy petting if we both moved to the other side of the door. She gazed at me for a moment, then swallowed hard. She said something I couldn't quite hear over the music.

5

"What?"

She leaned closer and I realized that the taut outline of her nipples was visible through the suit and the light coverup. "I don't have a lot of time."

Performance pressure, great, I thought, but she'd already gone inside the little room. Just as the door swung shut I found the light switch. I had it barely locked when I felt her hands on my shoulders.

"I don't know why I'm doing this," she said.

I surely didn't know why she was doing it either, but my heart was pounding. My reasons were about mood and need, that simple. I wanted to feel a woman against me, listen to her voice. I wanted to get my fingers wet.

"Are you sure?" Her eyes, a cloudy deep brown, were saying yes, but I needed to hear it. "I can unlock the door."

"I'm sure. I've always wondered . . . "

Our hands began to wander. I loved the feel of her hips under my palms. "Wondered what?" I nuzzled at her throat and inhaled the sweet scent of her hair. "Wondered what being fucked by a woman would feel like?"

Her skin jumped under my hands and I felt more confident knowing that I'd read her correctly. It was only then that I realized I had hoped she was somewhat experienced, because the thought of being touched by a woman was what had been circling my mind for the last few minutes. In my early days here, however, I'd learned that inexperienced straight women usually had no clue how to truly pleasure themselves, let alone another woman. Giving "feel that G-spot" lessons had ceased to be fun.

But I wouldn't say no at this point. It was all dyke ego, and I could live with the idea that there would be plenty of times when a guy would try his best and she'd think longing thoughts of the red-haired babe named Brandy at the resort, the one who had made her feel things she'd never felt before and hadn't felt since.

She was nodding while her hands stilled on my shoulders. She let me push her gently back against the heavy shelving where towels were stacked. My thigh went between her legs and we began to move to the pounding rhythm of the music that seeped under the locked door.

Her swimsuit was no challenge. I moved it out of my way, making room for my fingers and my mouth. She ground against my hip with a hiss as I stroked both nipples. They were erect and firm, and responded further to my tongue circling first one then the other.

I lifted my head to look into her eyes as I squeezed the reddened points. Her eyes widened as I increased the pressure to a pinch and she nodded, her mouth slightly open in surprise.

I kissed her throat while I teased and played with her nipples. She responded with more of her weight on my thigh, jerking against me to the beat of the music. I wanted her on my own rhythm, so I leaned away to study her eyes again.

Her hands had been passive on my shoulders, so I lifted one to the shelf support over her head. "I want you to hold on. Can you do that?"

"Yes," she breathed. She automatically brought her other hand up so both hands were firmly gripping the heavy metal frame. My fingers went back to her nipples with a sharp tug and she moaned loudly.

Her eyes were slightly glazed as I brushed her face with my hands. "It's all in the touch. We're not going to do anything you don't want."

"Okay . . . okay." She sounded nervous again.

"So you've wondered what it would be like. How is it so far?"

She nearly cracked a smile, which had been my intention. "So far, so good."

I pushed my thigh hard against her wet crotch and her responsive gasp sent a thrill of pure fire down my back. Maybe

I wasn't going to get touched in return, but feeling her move for me was already the highlight of the last month. "Just good?"

She nodded, and sexy, flirtatious Paige was suddenly back. "So far just good."

I arched an eyebrow. She gave me a look that said she dared me to try for more and I rose happily to the challenge. Another sharp tug at her nipples brought her focus back to her body, then I possessively grasped her by the waist, holding her still on my thigh.

"Nothing you don't want," I repeated.

She nodded frantically and tipped her hips up as I slid my hands under the back of her bikini bottoms to cup her supple ass. Soft skin over rock-hard muscle was just fine to hold and we began to move again, this time to the pace that I set.

"Do you want this?"

"Yes. I don't . . . have much time."

I didn't need the reminder. "Slow and sweet takes time, so we'll skip it. Is that okay?"

She whispered something as she arched her back and I asked her to say it again. Her cheeks reddened and her drawl was more pronounced. "I'm not here for slow and sweet."

"Tell me what you want." The air was close and musty and we were both starting to perspire. Her body felt increasingly hot against mine, bringing out a burning itch to say sweaty, hard words and finish like rockets. "You know you want to say it."

"Put your hand there."

"That's not what you want to say." I bit her lower lip as I squeezed her ass, hard. "What do you want?"

Her eyes were gleaming with desire as she looked down at our sweating bodies. "Make love to me."

"We're not making love here. We're strangers and we're going to have sex and walk away from each other. Isn't that it? Don't you want to get off with a strange woman? It's so forbidden, isn't it? It's slutty and wicked and it's going to feel so unbelievably good. This isn't about love, so say it."

She tightened her grip on the shelving, making her breasts taut against mine. "Yes, that's what I want. I want to get fucked by you, so fuck me—"

She sucked in her breath as I pulled the slick crotch of her bikini bottoms to one side and cupped her swollen cunt. Very few things ever felt this good to me, the combination of slippery skin and the one hard knot of engorged nerves. It had been a while since anything had felt that wonderful to my hand and I played with it all, dizzied by the hard throb between my own legs and the rising music of Paige's moans.

I went back to her breasts with my other hand while I enjoyed her writhing on my fingers and thigh. She was gasping little words—*good* and *please* and *more*—while I teased and further reddened her nipples.

"You are so hot, so fucking hot," I said, raising my voice to be sure she heard me. If we'd had more time I would have played more, let us both get higher, but quick was going to get her there. "Fucking hot and hot to fuck. Let's get this party started, baby."

My hand was covered with her excitement and one finger slipped easily inside her. She didn't have to moan "more" for me to arch my hand and shove two inside her, hard. With lube and lots of foreplay she might take more but right now two was plenty.

She ground down on my hand with a yelp the music hopefully covered. "That feels so good—harder! Just fuck me!"

I used my thigh behind my hand to give her what she wanted, grinning wildly because I'd found her G-spot, and the way her body was responding told me I might be the first. Everything was getting wetter and tighter as we strained against each other.

"Is this what you wanted?" I punctuated my words with hard strokes inside her. Lilac mingled with the scent of sex and she felt so very good against me.

She met every thrust. "Yes! More . . . "

"Don't let go. Hold on while I fuck you off your feet, just hold on."

My other hand went between her legs and two fingers slid to either side of her clit. Her cry might have been audible over the music, but then she was holding her breath. Her G-spot was suddenly very wet and rough and then her legs jerked.

She went rigid against me and then Paige, like a book, like a woman, Paige knew what she wanted. Her gaze locked with mine and she said through gritted teeth, "Don't . . . stop. Don't you fucking dare stop."

I didn't.

A few minutes later, after soft words and smooches, and mutual assurances that it had been unexpected and wonderful, we awkwardly peeled our bodies apart. It was a good thing we had plenty of towels at hand, but the gym had no showers.

Paige's drawl had a slow, lazy edge to it now. "I've never—I mean, I got so wet, I didn't know I'd do that."

"It's okay," I reassured her. "That's what you're supposed to do when everything gets touched the right way." She was flushed and I was doing inner cartwheels at the stunned look that remained in her eyes. She wasn't trying to retreat under a cool, sophisticated guise, as if what had just happened was just another passable orgasm in a long line of them.

With a stammer, she admitted, "I've read about it. I mean— I just didn't think I had a . . . "

"G-spot?" I caught myself before I teed off on the inferior skills of her previous lovers. Instead, I mildly said, "You do, honey. Believe me, you do."

"I can't go out like this. I—well." She blushed. "You know."

Her legs were sticky and fragrant. For that matter, so was my thigh. Two conditions I loved if there was time to do things all over again. "The people in the gym are only smelling their own sweat. Why don't we take a dip in the pool? It's a big pool, with lots of chlorine."

She nodded, still delightfully pink across her neck and shoulders. "Last one in is a—"

She didn't have to finish the sentence. I unbolted the door and we dashed around the row of elliptical trainers and out the door. She had her sandals off in no time, but I had to get out of my trainers. But it was still only a half-minute before we both were luxuriating in the deepest of the resort's pools.

We spluttered for a few moments, then she looked like she wanted to say something pointless like "thank you" or "you were good." Treading water, I said in a low voice, "It was what it was. Remember to always stretch before a workout."

She laughed in a wry, half-amused way, then swam to the ladder. The little coverup she wore clung to every single curve of her body and I took one last, long look. She gathered up her sandals and then she was gone.

I don't usually swim in my workout clothes so there was no way Tess didn't know what had delayed me inside the gym. I had patted down and partially dried while she finished her class, but my hair would be wet for some time. Vigorous toweling had it standing on end, and I hoped Tess was in the mood to lend me her hairbrush.

Tess's CD switched over to "I'm in Heaven," which I knew was the song that closed Body Pump for the hour. I grabbed a Bosu ball and dropped it flat side down and joined in. The thigh steps she'd mentioned were not a huge change, but I could see how the balance work standing on the half-dome "ball" would

11

benefit from it. A first-timer would be less likely to pull a sartorius muscle.

I was feeling mighty fine at the end of my short workout, and it must have showed because the first thing Tess said when we were mostly alone was, "Stop glowing."

"What?" I smoothed my hair with both hands, trying to tame the tangles.

Tess rummaged in her sport bag and came up with a hair tie. "Oh, hold still." She twisted a knot at the nape of my neck. I trusted her work; it wasn't the first time she'd tidied my unruly curl-infested mop. "Now wipe that innocent look off your face and tell me what happened in there."

"About what you'd expect."

"Did you get 'thanks, dahling, we must do lunch' or a voucher for a toaster oven?"

"More the latter, I think. I don't know." Mindful of the guests nearby, I lowered my voice. "She hadn't been with a woman before, that I'm pretty sure of."

"Oh, so you got, if you'll pardon the expression, stiffed?"

I swatted her. "I got what I wanted or I wouldn't have been there."

She gave me an intent look, then smiled slightly. "Okay. As long as that stays true, have fun."

"Speaking of getting what you want, how was Jean-Paul?"

Tess answered from the depth of her sport bag. Without looking up she handed me her hair spray. "Disappointing. All the looks, none of much else."

I coughed as I accidentally inhaled the spray. Scrunching my hair down, I asked, "What else were you looking for?"

She shrugged as I returned the spray and she zipped the bag closed.

"No, what? Tell me. Something didn't go right."

I fell into step next to her. We both had the next hour free, then she moved on to pool games while I gave much-needed relief to the KidZone staff.

"He was up for it, definitely." Her heavy sigh disquieted me. Tess preferred her sex with no strings, and once she hit it off with a guy the evening usually went fine from her perspective. Nobody owned her body but herself, and she took very good care of it.

"But you weren't?"

"He called me Tessie even when I asked him not to."

"Idiot."

"I kept thinking if he doesn't hear me about my name, is he going to hear me about what I like in bed? Been there, done that. Last night a vibrator was just easier."

I mentally reviewed the calendar, wondering where she was in her cycle. I didn't envy Tess her hormones, and she took loads of calcium and herbals to level out the cycle from hell. The Pill helped a lot, too, but still, there were times when she seriously needed some good sex and couldn't find anyone she trusted enough to take care of her. Except me.

It had been almost an accident, the first time we'd slept together. As we walked from the fitness center toward Village Square, I found myself recalling that night six . . . no, nearly seven months ago. I'd been here a year and a half by then. Tess and I had been buddies from the moment she greeted me next to the staff pool with, "Cool, another short woman who reads. That makes two of us."

She didn't care I was gay, I didn't care she was straight. We dished on the guests and management and shared the burdens of laundry and shopping. She knew all the sins of my past and that I didn't talk to my family. She'd lost her parents when she was seven, and I understood when she said she'd like a family, even one she wasn't speaking to. Tess let me borrow her car and I let her borrow my golf clubs, both of which were major displays of trust for each of us.

She'd knocked late one night with a half-bottle of red wine she'd smuggled out of the dining room. Holding it up to the light she said, "I can't seem to get laid, and I doubt this is enough to get drunk, but if you've got any chocolate my night will get better."

I scrounged for brownie mix and as soon as they were baking in the minuscule oven my quarters offered, we sat on the sofa—courtesy of Club Sandzibel decorators—and drank the wine.

It was July, and hot for the middle of the night. The air conditioner blowing on me felt good and the wine was the label served free to the guests—nondescript, but okay.

The last I had seen of Tess earlier that night she'd been happily sharing a cocktail with a broad-chested blond with a nice smile. "So what happened to that guest Romeo tonight?"

"He seemed nice until we were making out. I got scared."

It had happened before, her backing out. "You should trust your intuition."

"It's not exactly trustworthy this time of the month."

My hormones clicked along like clockwork and I'd never met a woman who said hers were as bad as Tess did. "You can't blame hormones for everything."

She didn't say anything and I finally glanced at her. She'd flushed a deep, angry red and the hand holding her wineglass was shaking.

"I'm sorry, that was a stupid thing to say." I sat up, kicking myself for being insensitive.

Her lips barely moved as she said, "If you were a man I'd have thrown my drink at you for that."

"I really am sorry, Tess."

"I don't *blame* my hormones for anything. I am only saying

that sometimes they make me irrational and I know it when it's happening. So I know not to trust myself and I take responsibility for what I do and say."

"I didn't mean it that way—"

"And there are days when it is all I can do not to snap at the guests or punch Randall in the stomach—"

"He deserves it—"

"And nights like tonight when I want to fuck like a rabbit. I thought you'd understand, but I guess you have to feel it to know what I'm talking about."

"I really am sorry, honey." I took the glass out of her shaking hand. "Tell me how I can help or at least make it easier."

"These are my feelings, Brandy, they're real. So don't make fun." Her face crumpled and hot tears filled her eyes.

"I will really try not to. That was a mean thing for me to say."

She was sobbing in earnest within seconds and I would have put my arms around her except she fended me off with a warning hand. Between gasps she managed, "It's just tension. I'm okay."

Feeling very helpless, I said, "It's only thirty minutes to brownies." She spluttered into her hands, which I took for a laugh.

After a minute I thought of tissues and fetched a box. She nodded thanks and blew her nose. When she'd calmed down a bit, she asked, "Have you ever needed to cry like that? Ever felt like if you didn't let something out you'd explode?"

I did understand that. "Sometimes, after really good sex. Not that I've had that in . . . a couple of years."

I was relieved to see Tess crack a little smile. "Lesbians are stupid if *you* can't have a good time."

"It's the freckles." Nobody had ever called freckles sexy. "Freckles and lack of opportunity. I think straight men are stupid

15

for the same reason about you." Tess wasn't exactly pretty, but her face—especially her smile—usually exuded an easy charm. Her eyes were her best feature, large and blue-gray. She had a swimmer's body, lean, light, and she bemoaned her slight tummy, which she called the Bane of Her Thirties. She was also smart and had a sense of humor, two big deals to me. But working here she rarely met a guy who cared. Not, it seemed, that she cared overmuch about their intelligence and wit either.

"I really thought I wanted that guy tonight, and maybe we would have had a good time. And then I realized I was hormonal. I get . . . " She flushed. "I get this . . . way. Like . . . "

I waited. The faint smell of cooking chocolate tickled my nose. Finally, when it seemed that Tess's flush was all embarrassment, I said, "What?"

"I get insatiable," she muttered. "I literally wear guys out."

A dozen things crossed my mind. First was, well, what was wrong with that? Then I realized that as a dyke I had all the equipment that might be up to taking care of an insatiable woman. I nearly made a joke then caught myself. I went for understatement. "That sounds frustrating." Then I couldn't help myself. "Especially with what I know about male anatomy. Granted, it's not much."

"*Frustrating* is one word for it. Thank you for not laughing."

I was doubly glad I hadn't. "I mean, what's so bad about having a, um, an appetite?"

"Don't suggest I try an orgy. I wouldn't feel safe. Dirk the Asshole did that."

"Damn me if I'll say anything Dirk the Asshole did."

"It's like—" Her voice broke. "I get there, climax, you know? More than once. And it's not enough. I want another one and I'm sure I won't get it, so I get anxious and try even harder. And then I feel like shit for picking up some guy to do me when I know he doesn't have a chance of satisfying me. A couple of

16

times I didn't take the time to be safe and believe me, waking up in the morning wondering if you've just contracted something fatal because you couldn't wait one minute for him to get a condom on . . . it's wretched. I respect myself and yet doing something like that is so self-destructive." She wiped her nose with the tissue and took several steadying breaths.

"I know what you mean," I said, and I did.

"I *hate* these hormones, Brandy. Because tomorrow I'll be fine." She dabbed at her eyes. "I'll be even better if I haven't made a fool of myself the night before, or let myself get hurt or used. I know that's true, and yet there's this screaming in my body that drowns all that out."

I nodded. "Like that night in college I told you about, when I got so drunk. I don't know what I was thinking, and I don't know what all I did. It was stupid getting drunk with people I couldn't trust." I felt a hot flush remembering a woman I'd thought was a friend handing me a health center pamphlet about STDs and suggesting, with a sneer, that I get tested. Tests were negative and nothing physically seemed wrong, so it was possible she was just fucking with my head—she turned out to be that kind of person—but I wasn't absolutely certain of what all I had done. And I felt stupid for putting myself in a position where I didn't know.

"How do I know I can trust somebody? If I let myself be truly open, and vulnerable? If I lose control and forget my name and just want more? And then say I'm sorry, it's just the one night a month I want it that way. How could anyone possibly cope with a cat in heat one night and one who just likes a nice petting and an easy screw the rest of the time?"

I didn't have an answer for her. It didn't seem like a guy who could do the one could also do the other, but maybe I was selling guys short. "I think you're right—the key is being safe while you hope you find the right person."

"It's not bloody likely," she said morosely. "Not working here, not with this dating pool."

The brownies were starting to smell really good and Tess seemed to have reached the end of her tears. "Are you talking about whips and chains?"

Tess, the woman I considered one of the most self-aware I'd ever met, was actually hanging her head. "No. I'm so embarrassed I'm even telling you about this. I'll be fine tomorrow. I just have to tough it out one night."

"Don't be embarrassed. I think everybody has something that's a little . . . not quite . . . ordinary in their sex life."

"Yeah? What's yours?"

I blushed.

"Oh, come on. I basically told you my whole thing and you won't share? I've freaked you out, haven't I?"

"For liking sex?"

"No. For liking it hot and endless and hard."

"Hell, Tess. Sometimes I like it hot and endless and hard, too. That's not the least bit bizarre to me." Our gazes met for a moment and then slid past each other. I suddenly felt very naked.

"So what were you blushing about?"

I realized that drawing it out would just make me seem prudish and unsophisticated. It wasn't that strange, at least I didn't think so. "I like two hands. Being touched from both the front and the back. While I'm standing."

Tess didn't snicker, but her eyes had a suspicious twinkle. "So, a chick with long arms."

Damn, the woman made me laugh. I felt sheepish. "Yeah, I guess. I don't know what it is about it, but I get shivers and I feel like I could just rub myself over her hands for days."

"Is that before, during or after the hot and endless and hard part?"

I shifted on the sofa. The air conditioning didn't seem to be working anymore. "Before. It's . . . I like teasing. Being teased."

Tess was nodding. "I like both sides of teasing. Doing and receiving."

"So that's my big secret." I finished the last bit of wine and wished I were the least bit drunk. "Spill your guts, Tess Carson, you're on *Candid Camera*."

She smiled, only slightly, then said in a low voice, "Most times I like sweet and kisses and touching that starts soft and then gets fierce, but not rough. I usually like being on top. I have more control. It lasts longer. But nights like tonight I want to be underneath a heavy body, and I want . . ." She swallowed. "I want something big. Inside. That was part of why I got spooked tonight when I realized I was hormonal. He wasn't big enough and I knew I was just going to end up crying and frustrated and he didn't deserve a night like that. To try and have me keep begging. I beg, Brandy, I beg, like some kind of junkie . . ."

She started to cry again and this time let me put my arms around her. "It must feel rotten." I could almost imagine it, having an itch in my cunt that wouldn't quit. I had times when I wanted to get laid, but it felt good, felt alive to me, even if a vibrator and a toy were my big date. "You've tried—on your own?"

"Hell, yes." She pushed me away with a deprecating laugh. "It's virtually impossible to hold yourself down and fuck yourself hard at the same time, you know? Even I can't satisfy me on a night like tonight."

She was making me think about how long it had been since I'd had good sex, since the other woman had really cared how I felt and what worked for me. Hot and endless and hard, with a lot of teasing to get me high—damn, but it sounded good. And I didn't know of a single lesbian within a hundred miles who could do that for me.

19

I laughed as I got up. The studio-style quarters meant she could follow my movements as I went to my nightstand. Pulling open the bottom drawer I ignored the vibrator and instead pulled out my favorite toy. "When you talk about big, what exactly do you mean?"

Tess gaped. "I can't believe you're showing me your dildo!"

Neither could I, actually. But I was intrigued and turned on. Tess and I had crossed some sort of line in our friendship. "I'm just curious."

Still giggling, she assessed the heavy silicon toy in my hands. "That's a very nice dildo you've got there."

"Tess, c'mon. I'm holding the thing until you tell me." It was very stylish, actually, with a marbled two-tone black and white swirl from top to bottom. But it was still a dildo and I felt funny just standing there with it. Like, hello, this is me and my friend the dildo.

"Oh, all right. That's usually a good size, I would think. About right. But tonight . . . "

"Okay, I get the picture." I tucked the toy back in the drawer. "Maybe you should just bring your own toy on a date."

"Oh, right," Tess said. "You really know nothing about the male ego."

"And I'm a bit proud of that," I admitted.

"And you've really never?"

"Nope. I've never even seen one, not even my brother's, in all the years since Stevie Watkins' peepee in the third grade. Trust me, I was far more impressed with Susan Porkland's breasts in the tenth grade."

She laughed, a genuinely hearty laugh, and I grinned back, glad that she seemed to be feeling better. I made a detour to the kitchenette area to check the brownies.

"Done," I pronounced. "They just need to cool a bit. I've got milk, I think."

"You think of everything. Sorry I've been a loon tonight.

Thank you for not freaking out. I'm really only like this for about twelve hours. Nobody agrees if it's an estrogen drop or a progesterone surge."

I set the brownie pan and a knife on the coffee table before I joined her again on the sofa. The warm aroma of chocolate was going right to my head.

I didn't know anything about raging hormones, but I had to admit, Tess did seem to know when hers were whacked, and she never did say anything like her hormones made her do it. I don't think I'd like feeling as if someone had slipped me a drug and I couldn't control my emotions or body, but everybody expected me to.

"I'm sorry I was rude earlier. About your hormones. I believe in them."

Her mouth hung open for a moment. "Oh. That's—nobody has ever said that before." I heard her swallow. "Thank you."

"Too bad we're nice girls, huh?"

"Speak for yourself!"

"Well, I meant . . . "

"What?"

What had I meant? "Nothing."

"Something. We've gone too far in baring our sexual souls to stop now."

"I was just thinking, well, you like to tease and be on top and I like it when the woman I'm with does that with me. And I could fuck you for hours if that was what you wanted sometimes. Hold you down and . . . "

The air between us was suddenly thick and I couldn't breathe it in. I was incredibly aroused at the thought of taking care of Tess's itch. If she'd needed a backrub I'd have given it without a second thought. How was this different?

She took a sharp breath. "What are you suggesting, Brandy?"

I was still stunned by my own audacity. Maybe the brownie

smell was releasing some sort of inhibition reducer. I felt just a bit dizzy.

In the pages of the many old and new lesbian anthologies stacked on my bookshelf, women were having sex with strangers, in threesomes, in embassy bathrooms, at the top of the Statue of Liberty, with hoards of biker daddies and bevies of stiletto-wearing femmes. They were playing out fantasies with costumes, ropes and all manner of toys and though some of it wasn't what I dreamed about in my most outlandish fantasies, it all still sounded good. Alive, free, sensual and, most of the time, very loving. Taking care of each other, whatever that meant.

Like, do unto her what she wants, so that she may do unto you what you want.

"Fuck buddies," I said. "We can be fuck buddies."

We never did eat the brownies that night. In a mix of laughter and nerves we'd cleaned toys and fetched towels. I hadn't really thought we'd go through with it, but when we'd stood there, next to my bed, accessories laid out in almost clinical precision, Tess had pushed the hair back from my face.

Leaning close, her fingertips had feathered down my shoulders and arms. There was no turning back after she asked, in a husky voice, "So, you like to be teased?"

"Who's that?"

I nearly knocked Tess down and had to grab her hip for balance. We'd almost reached the main reception plaza, and she'd stopped right in front of me. The brief contact made me flash on our last night together. It had been nearly a month—too long, at least for me. And after Paige, well, the thought of Tess's hands cupping me had me tingling. We had agreed, Tess and I, that as fuck buddies we only sought each other out in dire need. I was getting there.

"I know that woman from somewhere."

I could only see her back now. For a new arrival she was early in the day. Though the guests leaving and guests arriving overlapped for several hours, rooms wouldn't be ready until the current occupants left. She had a ton of luggage, too. She was tall, thin like a bicyclist, and her kinked black hair was cropped short to a shapely scalp. "I don't know. I can't see her face."

I belatedly realized I was still holding onto Tess's waist. I reluctantly let go. Touching her felt really good. It always did.

"Oh—she's turned around."

"That's Celine Griffin," I said automatically. Holy shit, I thought. Celine Griffin.

"Who?"

"She's a comic, a lesbian stand-up comic. She was on Leno. Cover of some magazines."

"Oh—she must be with the Ladies on Vacation group."

"Huh?" I remembered seeing the group booking on the weekly info sheet, but I rarely took the time to read those. I didn't need to. People would easily tell you all about themselves. Being a good listener was one of my strengths.

Tess gave me a look like I was stupider than a bag of hammers. "I knew you'd missed it. You duck the meetings and don't read the sheet. Probably just as well because you'd have been driving me nuts in anticipation."

"What *are* you talking about?"

"Ladies on Vacation is a lesbian tour group. There's more than three hundred of them arriving today. They booked the whole resort."

The hair on the back of my neck stood on end. "No way."

"Way." Tess smirked. "I nearly pointed it out to you but I thought you could use a big surprise. Though I guess if you'd known about it, you might have been more selective this morning."

Lesbians. Not straight women dabbling in what they felt was kinky. Not curious first-timers wondering if they'd prefer the other side. Lesbians, bona fide, already-know-what-to-do-with-a-clit lesbians.

My entire body, only recently recovered from wishing Paige had had a thought about what I might like, abruptly felt swollen.

Tess was assessing me with a kind, familiar gaze. "I thought you'd be pleased."

"Nothing I did this morning takes the edge off what I could do tonight," I said. My voice had gotten raspy and my mouth was dry.

"You have a real good time, then," Tess said as she resumed walking toward Village Square. "Just play safe, as you always say to me."

We skirted Celine Griffin's impressive collection of suitcases. I was trying not to stare at the celebrity when I saw Paige bearing down on me. She still wore her swimsuit and coverup. With a sinking feeling I realized she had something small in her hand, and I knew what it probably was.

Tess veered off with a cheery, "See you later."

I smiled a welcome at Paige and gritted my teeth for the inevitable.

The silence was awkward. Then Paige held out the small jeweler's box, emblazoned with the logo of the Club Sandzibel Boutique.

"I wanted to get you something."

"You didn't have to." I was cringing inside. Paige had not thought this through.

"I—I wanted to. Nothing like that has ever happened to me and I just wanted to make it, I don't know, special."

"Really, Paige, I can't. It was . . . special, yes, but . . . "

"If you don't like it you can take it back. Get something else, or the cash, or whatever . . . "

I tried not to let a smolder of anger show. "If I do that what does that make me?"

She blew out her breath and I realized the thought had never occurred to her. "I'm sorry. I'm not trying to pay you or something. I'm just trying to thank you." She didn't seem pissed or sad, just confused about what to do.

"I know." I would have hugged her if there hadn't been so many people around. "Whatever that is, why don't you keep it for yourself? To remember something unexpected. And remind yourself that you have—" I realized the man I spotted approaching us was her boyfriend. "To remind you that you have choices." I glanced meaningfully over her shoulder.

She straightened nervously and her drawl broadened again, but it wasn't the least bit lazy. "Some things never occurred to me. That's what I'm trying to thank you for."

"I understand, Paige. So keep the memory. And the memento."

She closed her eyes for a moment, then nodded. She turned away just as her boyfriend arrived. He was not a happy man. Glancing at the box in Paige's hand, he snapped, "Found jewelry you liked then?"

"Yes, as a matter of fact." The last thing I heard her say was, "I'm not going to apologize again for not wanting to get married . . ."

"Sounds like you won a toaster oven."

The sardonic observation came from behind me, and I turned to find myself the object of Celine Griffin's attention. On TV and videotape she looked elegant and cool. In person, even with a fine glimmer of perspiration at her hairline, she looked ten times more elegant, twenty times more cool and fifty times more sexy. Something about the deep cocoa of her skin made me want to go on staring at her. Defined shoulders highlighted a collarbone I had, from time to time, fantasized about licking.

I wondered if, just by studying my expression, she could tell I had a framed magazine cover with her face on it in my quarters. That was where Tess knew her from. I'd have to take it down before Tess saw it or she'd never give me any peace. I tried for humor. "Not the first one."

"I'll bet." She gave me a close once-over and I wished I hadn't gone swimming in my workout clothes. Then I remembered my hair was a shambles and at that point I was certain I was blushing.

Celine Griffin—ask anybody—has the most incredible eyes, a dark blue with yellow rings. In her hourlong cable special a few years back, she'd acknowledged them as a legacy from a Caribbean slave owner seven generations back.

"You work here?"

"Yes." Belatedly, I remembered that I did, indeed, have a job to do. "Welcome to Club Sandzibel. Do you have any questions about the all-inclusive nature of our program?"

She shook her head, looking amused at my practiced speech. "I've been to other clubs, just not this property. What's your specialty?"

I laughed. "How should I answer that?" Her eyes went cool and I realized my tone had been suggestive. But then, I had thought her question was flirtatious. Hiding a nervous gulp, I quickly added, "Circus tumbling and occasional onstage ham. But mostly stretching, and several daily fitness routines."

She looked me up and down again and her eyes implied she liked what she saw. "I can tell."

Confused by the hot and cold in her flirting, I didn't quite know how to respond. "I lead a Bosu ball Body Pump class at two, if you want to plunge into activities. A lot of guests prefer to start slow, however."

"I'll try to remember." Again, she gave me a lazy appraisal. I was starting to wonder if she had an unconscious tic that made her look at all women like she was planning to take them to bed. Or maybe it was me. After all, I was chatting casually with Celine Griffin and by tonight there would be lesbians all around me. This was in addition to the steady throb between my legs left over from Paige and thinking about that first, incredible night with Tess.

I flailed about for something to say and retreated into work mode. "Has someone made arrangements for your bags to be taken to your room?"

"I believe so, but thank you. Is your name really Brandy?"

"It really is. Coincidence that it matches the hair."

"Was it hard to grow up with that name?"

I shrugged. "It's short for Brandywine. I haven't had the guts to ask my mom if that's what she was drinking the night I was conceived."

She laughed so heartily that heads turned. Since I suspected the answer was yes, it really wasn't a joke to me, but other people always did laugh because they didn't know my parents the way I did. "It gets worse."

"How?"

"My last name is Monsoon."

"Oh, no way."

"Way."

"And is that indicative of anything in your personal nature?" The flirtatious twinkle in her eyes was very pronounced. Her sheer white tank top set off her skin to perfection and if I stared, which I realized was exactly what I was doing, I could see that her nipples were even darker than the rest of her sleek skin. Darker, and slowly hardening—watching them rise was bewitching.

I felt on uncertain ground with her, and other staff were lis-

27

tening. I played it safe with, "Come to Bosu ball at two and I might answer that."

She quirked an eyebrow as if to say I'd scored a point in the flirtation game. I nodded with what I hoped was a sultry kind of cool, instead of the dizzy, bemused way I actually felt, and headed for my quarters. I needed a shower, a very cold shower.

Chapter Two

In the chaos of my studio apartment I found the tour group update sheet for the coming week. The group was called LOVE. I felt stupid for not having seen the opening lines. *The "Ladies" on Vacation Enterprises could also be "lesbians." The resort will see 312 female guests and their families in buildings A, B and E. Buildings C and D will be unoccupied; expect maintenance and carpet layers. Entertainment provided by LOVE. We are advised most are couples and should be treated as such. Male staff are cautioned to avoid the appearance of flirting or staring, and all staff are advised to be additionally sensitive to avoidance of sexual or sexist jokes, even in adult-only settings . . .*

Three hundred and twelve lesbians. They were going to be the only guests we had. Okay, maybe most of them were in couples, but surely one of them might be interested in a short but trim, red-haired woman who, among other things, could improve their golf game. I realized I felt about as giddy as I had the one time I'd gone to the Dinah Shore Classic. This year's tournament had been just a few weeks ago, and if I could have afforded it I might have gone, pining for lesbian company as I was. How good was life that instead of my having to find a landscape of lesbians, they'd found me? Damn. Life was *very* good.

After a change of clothes, a losing battle with my hair and a quick pit stop at the lunch buffet for an apple, I headed for the other end of the resort toward the KidZone. Of course it was a longer route to go by reception on the way, but I couldn't resist.

I saw Dykes, with a capital D, Dykes and Dykes and Dykes. I felt like a kid at a picnic.

Hot Dykes, I like hot Dykes, I sang to myself. *This kind of girl likes tasty hot Dykes. Fat ones, short ones, Dykes that climb on rocks. Femmie ones, butch ones, and maybe Dykes with strap-on co—*

"Brandy, can you lend a hand with the queue?" Randall interrupted what I thought was an inspired commercial jingle for lesbian delights, but Randall had been put on this earth to squelch all the fun out of my life.

"I've got a couple of minutes before Rhea's expecting me."

I helped Sarah and Steffie from Sausalito find their room keys and explained the weekly calendar while reiterating their freedom to do whatever they liked.

"You mean we can just go down to the beach and get snorkeling gear any time?"

"When the snorkel hut is open, during these hours." I pointed out how to read the color coding. "And there are daily lessons at ten, so you might want to sign up to be sure to get a spot."

Linda and Libby from Lynchburg promised they'd meet me tomorrow for Morning Stretch. June and Jody from Juneau were eager to try sailing, while Deena and DeeDee from Dayton couldn't wait to stay in their room all week, nudge

nudge. Then Mary and Tina from Spokane completely blew my alphabet fun, but they were dumping their bags in the room and heading for the nearest pool.

That's when I remembered that phrase from the weekly sheet: *Most are in couples*. Hell, they were *all* in couples, it seemed to me. It was a great jazz to have so many lesbians around me but so far I wasn't getting any heat from them. The heat was all on my side and I was certainly feeling it.

As I walked the rest of the way to the KidZone I pondered the ethical dilemma. I had few qualms about spending some quality moments with an entangled straight woman who sought me out and made the first definitive moves. But would I feel the same about an entangled lesbian? It seemed unsisterly to the other lesbian to fool around with her girlfriend, even if I had an engraved invitation to do so. Well, I would have to give that a lot of thought if the situation arose.

I hate ethical dilemmas and the older I got the more they dogged me, it seemed. At twenty I wouldn't have asked about entanglements. By the time I was thirty, I thought morosely, I'd be limiting myself to women who were looking for a commitment. How deadly dull that would be.

A small imp inside me wondered briefly what I would do if both women in a couple wanted to fool around, then realized the answer was a resounding Yes, Yes and Yes. Oh goodness, I didn't need to think about such things at that moment.

Then I remembered Celine Griffin, who as far as I knew was single, and thought maybe I didn't need to be worrying over-much about my options for threeways and stolen hours with roaming girlfriends. Maybe some open one-on-one dinner-dancing-flirting-lovemaking nights might be in my future. I wouldn't make the mistake of thinking it was the beginning of something, but it would be far more than I had had in a very long while.

~ళ~

One of the attractions of the Sandzibel property is daylong childcare, and though I liked kids, I did not envy the staff who worked there at all. For every great, curious, interesting kid there are two that snivel and cry about everything. And every sniveler had an overprotective mother who just wouldn't let the kid have fun. The programs were very safe, and well-staffed. We got bumps and bruises, and that included from the circus camp for the older kids, but that was all.

The sun was starting to heat up the cement near the lap pool, and sunbathers were slathering on the sunblock. Saturdays were always a little different because the previous week's guests were allowed to linger, dine and use the facilities until they needed to depart for flights later in the day. The new guests would rub shoulders for a while with the old. Women were already pulling loungers side-by-side, and I shivered for a moment, anticipating the poolside landscapes of the coming week.

"We were here the wrong week," I heard one of the male guests say to his poolside chum. "Major babe-o-rama."

His buddy, obviously quicker on the uptake, said back, "Go ahead, hit on one. I'll sew you back together."

I kept my chuckle to myself and arrived at the KidZone security gate to find Rhea listening patiently to a mother explain how her ten-year-old darling shouldn't try tumbling at circus camp because he could break a nail or something.

Rhea, clad in shorts and a club T-shirt, didn't look as if she was waiting to hear that her dissertation, "Mutton on Monday: Deconstruction of Food in the Novels of Jane Austen," had been accepted at the University of Southern Florida and she could officially append Ph.D. to her name. The mother was particularly shrill and Rhea did have, around the edges, a look like she couldn't believe this was all an advanced English degree had brought her so far. She needed a break.

At least my college work was in phys. ed. and I was actually doing that for a living, sort of. As fun as it was, I acknowledged, this was ultimately a dead-end job. I was hoping, with my good evaluations, to get moved to non-U.S. locations and see more of the world. Tess said the lifespan of a guest services representative with Club Worldwide, Inc., was about six years. I realized that she had to be in about year five. I wondered, before two toddlers grabbed my knees, what that would mean for her. For our . . . friendship.

Then I realized I was thinking about career prospects, and not ten minutes earlier I'd been musing about commitment and relationships and ethical dilemmas. Three hundred lesbians and that's what they brought out in me? It was pathetic!

"Well, how about we let him try just today—he really wants to. Carly and Adam will keep a very close eye on him," Rhea was saying. "And this is Brandy, one of the tumbling instructors."

I nodded encouragingly. "It teaches confidence and balance and they all love it."

The boy in question chimed in with, "Please, Mom? I'll be careful."

Another woman I had thought belonged to a different kid spoke up. "Sweetie, he's old enough. And he'll feel rotten to sit out when everyone else is having fun. You and I can sit by the pool and have a daiquiri for the first time in eleven years. That's why we're here."

Moms, they were lesbian moms. I grinned ear to ear and felt a strange but pervasive sense of pride. Wow. My people were here this week, and some of them were *moms*.

I was set upon by the toddlers again, and this time I gave chase. We'd had a running battle all week and it was time to show these desperadoes who was the law. That would be me, Sheriff Monsoon.

I hadn't quite proven my superiority when their parents came to claim them for a last good-bye. One protested it wasn't Saturday yet, while the other said I was the best playmate ever. Rhea had eagerly headed over for her lunch, so I got the gooey parting hugs and smooches from several more of the kids before she got back. I have to say that part of the job is pretty cool. Kids give great hugs.

My hour ended, I went back for a more substantial lunch, passing Tess and others in the main pool lustily lampooning *Titanic*. Various superheroes were called on to save poor Kate Winslett (played convincingly by Tess) from Jaws, the Pool Shark. I always wanted Kate to save herself, but Alicia—trapeze artist extraordinaire—was a treat to view in a Wonder Woman costume. It was the boots and the bustier that always made me sigh.

When I realized most of the Ladies of LOVE were ogling Wonder Woman, too, I grinned so hard my face hurt.

This was going to be a fabulous week.

Mid-afternoon on the Florida Gulf Coast can be muggy, overcast and hot. The first Afternoon of the Lesbians, as Rhea had termed it earlier, was no exception. The front had moved in quickly, and would soon move on, but the low rumble of off-shore thunder was probably the reason why nobody showed up for the two p.m. Body Pump class.

Nobody but Celine Griffin, that is.

"Not at all," I assured her when she asked if I minded doing a class for one. "I'd be happy to customize it for you. Is there any area you'd like to concentrate on this week?"

She regarded me with that clear blue-yellow stare. "What do you think?"

At one time that question would have thrown me into a regular tizzy. Few women or men like to be told their tummy or butt or thighs need toning. Diplomacy was required. Celine Griffin, however, wasn't just anybody. She was somebody I would seriously like to have dinner with later. More than dinner. Something better than diplomacy was needed.

I walked slowly around her while she regarded me with amused tolerance. "You've worked hard on your abs and glutes, it shows. How's your back—any pain or stiffness?"

"No, not since I added a rigorous ab routine to my workout."

"Your trainer is good. You've got great all-around tone. If you want, we could do squats and lunges after a general workout. Thighs primarily, but great for calves and lifting the glutes."

"At my age, my glutes can use all the lifting they can get."

"Great." I risked a direct look. She was smiling. Okay, then. On went the music, up went our weights and for the next twenty minutes we worked out without saying more than necessary. I knew she was forty-five and I'd done the math. Nineteen years older than I was. I hoped I looked that good at forty-five. I tried to picture myself nearly twenty years in the future and it was impossible. The only thing I knew was that I wouldn't be working at this job. Personal Trainer to the Stars had a nice ring to it. Maybe I'd invent some new fitness craze and make millions selling the DVDs. *Brandy Monsoon's All-Weather Workout* or something like that.

On my third set of French lifts, I wondered what Tess saw in her future. As if my thoughts had conjured her up, Tess arrived, her hair still wet from the pool games.

"I thought I'd see if you were free, but you're both working hard, aren't you?"

"She's a sadist," Celine muttered between grunts.

I grinned. Celine was loving every minute, I could tell. "We're about to start some Bosu lunges."

"I've had enough of those for the day," Tess said. She gave me an inquiring look. Celine turned to pick up her towel and I answered Tess with a shrug.

Tess hesitated and I remembered her earlier offer. That was before I knew about the arrival of LOVE and I was pretty sure I didn't need to bother her for . . . help. If it wasn't Celine Griffin it would be somebody. Tess nodded brightly, like she understood, but there was a flash of something else as she took leave of us. As excited as I was by the thought of spending a night with a lesbian doing very lesbian things, I felt the strangest pang watching Tess walk away.

Vividly in my head I could hear her voice from the first night we were together. "So," she had said, "you like to be teased."

I breathed out a choked yes and for the next hour Tess stroked, nibbled, massaged and brushed every inch of my body except my breasts, inner thighs and cunt. I was high on her attention and all of the sensation. My heart was pounding so hard my vision blurred. Part of the time she held me against the wall, then finally she let me stretch out on the bed. I don't know how long she swept my back with her hair but my breathing was so rapid I was dizzy.

"Brandy," she finally whispered, very tenderly. "I don't know when you've had enough. I can do this for a long time, and I'm loving it, but I need to you tell me when you want me to fuck you."

My entire body jerked in response. "Now, now," I stammered. I was so wet I could smell it. Nobody I'd ever been with had made me wait so long. Maybe, I had thought somewhat irrelevantly, if Tess was gay she wouldn't have been able to wait.

"Brandy?"

To my chagrin I realized Celine Griffin was looking at me expectantly. Hell, I'd forgotten where I was in the workout. I shouldn't be thinking about Tess, anyway. I realized I was wet, again, still, continuously it seemed today. "Sorry, I was thinking what would be best next. Bosu ball?"

"I have no idea what that is."

I showed her the half-dome workout balls and we practiced balancing on them. "You can just stand on the ball for five minutes and you won't believe how many little muscles you have to use. Using them will help them define and compact."

"This is amazing," she agreed. "I bet I'm sore tomorrow. Especially my feet."

"Sign up for a massage," I suggested.

Celine gave me a look that made something deep down inside me clench. "Do you give massages?"

"Not officially," I said, then I firmly directed her into lunges. My entire body was screaming loudly that I wanted to get horizontal, vertical, diagonal, perpendicular, it didn't matter, as long as we both got very thoroughly satisfied, but I didn't want her to know that. Yet.

We were both drenched by the end of the forty-five-minute workout. "Be sure to drink a lot of water while you're here. The humidity just soaks it out of you and dehydration can level you in less than a day."

"Thanks." She slung a towel around her neck, and it framed her collarbone. We stared at each other and I felt next to naked. When I picked up my Bosu ball to stow in the large locker, she followed suit.

I leaned into the locker to get the ball into the best position so the door would close. The locker was large enough for mats and barbells, but the Bosu balls were stressing its limits.

A wave of tingling goose pimples swept over me as Celine leaned in too, her body the length of mine. In my ear she said, "Here's the other one."

I shuddered. Her pelvis rocked against my ass. Part of me couldn't believe this was happening—Celine Griffin!—while the rest of me had stopped thinking at all. I choked back a moan but couldn't stop my hips from moving in response to her.

The open door sheltered us temporarily and Celine had no doubt noticed that. Again, her low voice melted into my ear. "I think I'm not the only one who'd like a massage."

We strained against each other for several heartbeats, then I moaned and pushed back against her. She was rolling my muscle shirt up my body and my sport bra went with it. I felt a pang of alarm and stiffened, then her hands lifted both of my breasts so that her fingers could pull firmly on my bare nipples.

I moaned, loudly, and, completely stunned, I felt a clenching inside my cunt that was very close to climax. First Paige, and now being touched by someone who obviously knew her way around a willing female body—I was in a serious state of need.

I had all my weight on my hands and I didn't want her to stop, but just as the inner "you're gonna lose your job, you idiot," alarms got loud enough for me to hear she was rolling my bra and shirt back down and stepping away.

My knees nearly buckled. I took several deep breaths, aware that I was blushing, hard, but finally I turned to face her.

"Have dinner with me," she said. Thunder rumbled in the distance.

It was just lust, I told myself, looking at those amazing yellow-ringed blue eyes. Lust was fine with me. "I'm free at six-thirty, then there are skits and introductions at eight."

"Oh, I'd forgotten about the greeting falderal." She gave me a somewhat sheepish look. "And I have to have dinner with the tour people. I'm tour group staff, technically. I'd forgotten about that, too. What about a drink at ten?"

"That would be . . . great."

She stepped closer and I couldn't breathe. "You are the hottest woman I've seen in a long time. I intend to seduce you."

With a slow blink I hoped looked sultry or sexy or alluring or anything except achingly needy, I said, "You already have."

She was pleased. It showed in her eyes. "Until ten, then. What do you drink?"

"Whatever you're pouring."

"How do you like your sex?"

"With women." I was feeling more confident by the minute.

"I presumed that." She moved so close that her lips were nearly on mine. The thunder was moving closer. "I can cook in a wide range, but only what's on your menu."

I realized what she was asking and I didn't think I could pull off the sophistication of a string of acronyms and code words like in a personal ad.

My hesitation I'm sure spoke volumes, because she quickly added, "Given the reaction of that woman this morning, I do find it hard to believe you're not a little bit adventurous."

I blushed. "I, um—I'm not shy, but I'm not edgy either. Pain is a turnoff."

Her lips twitched. "Considering the workout you just put me through, I wouldn't have said that."

I laughed a little. "That's not the kind of pain I mean. There's nothing alarming about . . . stretching. Sensation is different from pain."

She nodded and all the humor left her eyes. I felt as if she were peeling me open. "I like to be in control, Brandy. That's what I'm trying to say. Will that be difficult for you?"

I sighed with some relief. "No. It should be okay. As long as . . . " I blushed.

"Finish the thought," she said firmly. "It's important."

"As long as I get to touch you back. That's, like, half the deal for me."

She laughed her lovely, throaty laugh, warm and truly amused. "Half the deal for me, too. I may be a bit of a top, but I'm not stone."

I joined her in laughter, and my foolish heart felt a twinge that was wholly inappropriate to the situation. Celine Griffin would leave next Saturday and I would still be here. But laughing with her, feeling at ease even when I was completely turned on and distracted by visions of me on her bed, it felt wonderful. We spoke each other's language. and though many of my fellow staffers were fun and friendly, the other gay staffers were all men. Tess was the only one I really let go with, in laughter. And in sex, I reminded myself. Laughter and sex—there wasn't much more to happiness than that.

"I have to shower and change," I said reluctantly. "And then I have another hour at KidZone and a fitness staff meeting."

"Work's a bitch, isn't it?"

"Yeah, but it beats being unemployed."

It was very awkward for just a moment and I admitted to myself that I didn't quite know what to do. We'd agreed to have sex later, but how did I say good-bye until then? Pretend European casualness with a cheery *au revoir*? Shaking hands was right out.

Experience must have rewards, because Celine did exactly the right thing. She picked an imaginary hair off my shirt, then smoothed her hand lightly down my front. "Until later, then. I am looking forward to tonight with you." At least it was the right thing until she added, "I'm sure it will be memorable."

She walked away and I pondered why I felt a sudden chill. Wasn't a night of abandoned sex with Celine Griffin—bona fide lesbian—what I wanted? And wasn't it a little bit late to be wondering what constituted "memorable" for her? Did I want to be merely memorable? It had seemed more than enough with Paige and the many like her, but with another dyke . . . why did that seem inadequate?

I was halfway back to my quarters when the thunder broke overhead. Rain hissed over the concrete and landscaping, feeling wonderful on my skin. I was thinking too much, I decided. Fuck now, think later.

As far as my schedule went, it had been a typical Saturday. Randall spent the fitness staff meeting explaining how expensive the equipment was, then airing two complaints from the previous week. The first simply said that "that girl who teaches aerobics is rude." That narrowed it down to four of us, but none of us was taking credit. Any chance remark might have been taken the wrong way. Usually when I meant to be rude, I made sure people remembered my name.

The other complaint was that the music in the fitness center was too loud. We all blamed the volume on guests. Yes, we solemnly agreed that from now on if we observed that the music was too loud, we would turn it down to a manageable level. I recalled how the loud music that morning had covered the sounds Paige and I had made. Randall caught me smiling and treated me like a four-year-old by making me say, "Yes, sir, I think complaints are important."

"Not a word about the other two hundred people in our program last week, none of whom complained," I muttered to Tess as we left.

"I've heard a delicious rumor that Randall is getting transferred to Barbados."

"Oh, that would be great, not that he deserves it. Except with my luck I'd get transferred there, too."

Tess stopped walking for a moment. Village Square was just

beyond us, and the early evening gathering of guests before dinner was underway. "Do you want to get transferred?"

"Eventually," I said. "I took this job to see the world, remember?"

"Yeah," Tess said. "I was just checking that you hadn't changed your mind." She abruptly hurried again toward the dining room. "There won't be any chocolate bread left."

"Especially with so many women here this week." So many lovely women, I thought, skirting women holding hands with each other or their children.

"*Hola*, Brandy," I heard from several of the kitchen staff as I slipped in to see if there was more spinach to fill the empty bowl at the salad bar. If not, I'd settle for romaine.

Cruz, who lived with his elderly mother and two equally elderly aunts, handed me a small bowl of freshly cut pineapple chunks, which I adore. From what I could follow in Spanish, he was saying thank you for my taking the time to write down some simple exercises that might help his mother's recently sprained ankle. I saw Jesus heading to the front with a fresh bowl of spinach and followed him quickly out of the kitchen before Rudy—prima donna master chef—saw me.

Tess had settled at a remote table where more staff people would eventually gather. We were free to dine with guests and otherwise mingle, but Saturdays the food was a little bit better than usual, while time was short before we were all required to be on hand for introductions. I scarfed down the raw spinach topped with ahi warmed in a basil marinade, then dug into the chocolate bread. "Thanks for not stealing my bread."

"You're welcome," Tess answered. There was no honor when it came to chocolate bread. She pointed with her fork as she munched on chicken and broccoli. "This week's tour staff. Those are the owners in the lead, and some of the entertainers. Well, I think you already know that, don't you?"

I followed her gesture and saw a party of eight women—my

42

gaydar pinged eight distinct times, which felt wonderful—to a private table in the corner. One of them was Celine Griffin.

"So," Tess said brightly. "Got a date yet?"

"Tonight," I answered. I studied Celine's elegant, lean figure before she disappeared into the general manager's dining room, and remembered the feel of her along my back. My entire body goose-pimpled.

"That didn't take long."

I glanced at Tess, and then blushed in response to Tess's knowing look. "We, um, settled things earlier."

"I thought you might." Tess's expression was exceedingly cheerful. "You seemed to be clicking."

"I hope we do."

"I meant it," she said. "I'd . . . "

I realized what Tess was referring to, and I wasn't sure why she was bringing it up. "I know you would. I didn't want to bother . . . I mean, since Celine is . . . "

"More than capable, I'm sure. And your type. I understand." Tess took a big bite out of her slice of chocolate bread.

I felt confused but I didn't know why, which just confused me more. I tried to lighten the air with a jest. "Well, whether she's my type remains to be seen, I guess."

"Just be safe, okay? I've got to shower and change," she announced, pushing back her chair. She wrapped the rest of her dessert in a napkin. "Did you want to demo stretching tonight?"

I nodded, taken aback by her abrupt departure. Tess was telling *me* to be safe? That was usually my line to her. "Yeah, it's easiest."

"I imagine the women will like it," Tess added. To my relief she was smiling in her usual way.

"I imagine." I winked at her and she looked about to say something, then headed off at high speed toward the dining room's rear exit.

I noticed more than one head turning as Tess went by. Men

had always drooled over Tess, but this time there were several women with their tongues out and I felt very strange, very strange indeed.

I'd had time to shower earlier so didn't have to hurry anywhere before the evening entertainment. Clad in my usual Club Sandzibel muscle shirt, black biking shorts, club blue socks and white cross-trainers, I queued up with the other staffers in the main hall where all guests would gather for the orientation to the club and introductions. I was planning to slip in to see the pianist-singer-comic who would perform. We were all getting quite a treat, being entertained instead of the other way around. Celine Griffin was doing standup on Friday. It would be more lesbian-specific entertainment than I'd seen in the past half-decade.

Tess arrived just in time, her hair slightly damp at her scalp, but otherwise looking elegant as always. The lights went down as Randall, general manager and all-around jerk, took the stage.

In the dark I let myself think about what the night would be like with Celine Griffin. Sex was on my mind and it was hard to stop considering it. I realized then that Tess's light, sexy cologne was wafting from her and I was practically taking hits off of it. I abruptly wanted Tess to pull me into the nearest private room and have me. I was wet and I could again hear her saying, "So, you like to be teased."

It was Celine I was going to be with, not Tess. Celine was a lesbian. Tess was straight. Damned good in bed, sensitive, caring, compassionate, loyal, Tess was a friend. A buddy. Not a lesbian. I recalled with a shiver that shook my composure how I had choked out my begging plea that first night. I'd had enough teasing and I needed her inside me.

She had fucked me from behind, with her fingers. I'd come

fast and hard, my ears ringing with my choking moans, then felt her part my swollen lips with the tip of my favorite toy. She slid it inside me and muscles I hadn't known I had gave way with a gush of wet that made Tess gasp out, "Yes, you like that, don't you?"

I put my face in the pillows and spread my knees so I could take the toy deep. Tess paused for a moment when I groaned.

"Do you like it all the way in?"

"Yes, don't stop!"

"Hard? Or slower?"

"Slower, but all the way."

Her hair was on my back and it felt fabulous. We moved together for a long time and I became increasingly incoherent. Tess was going to take care of me, and it was as good as I'd ever had. As good as anyone had ever felt inside me. It was the same toy as always, I thought with bemusement. Same toy and yet Tess made it different. Better, somehow.

I needed to climax and I was nearly there. When I get close I can get anxious that it won't happen, that I'll get stuck turned on and high and not get the release. I put my weight on one elbow and reached between my legs with my hand.

"Let me," Tess said. "I wasn't sure . . . let me do that."

Our fingers tangled over my clit. I stroked past it several times, not quite touching, then Tess pushed my hand away. "Like that," I gasped.

"You really like to be teased, don't you? Touched near, around, against, but not right on it, yes?" Her finger circled my engorged clit. "I like to tease, but it is so incredibly hot to tease you while I fuck you, to do both at once."

I cried out and felt the contractions start. My clit was throbbing between Tess's fingers and she pulled me back into her arms, impaling me fully on the toy. I came on her thigh, quaking in her arms. Some minutes later I realized we were coiled on the bed in a heap, both sweating, and the scent of her cologne was all over me.

Tess nudged me to move up in line and I snapped out of my triple-X reverie. Moments later we were introduced as part of the "energetic, fitness-for-fun trainers!" The boys always went first—sailing and waterski pros, then the golf pro, tennis pro, and finally those of us who taught fitness and circus training. I never thought it was coincidence that the boys were in jobs with "pro" commonly added to them. I knew it meant they had competed professionally, but still, it could rankle, especially when their hours weren't as strenuous as mine.

The "pros" faded to the background and a burst of "Tribal Dance" sent Jerry, Rajid and me tumbling across the stage, followed by Tess, Moika and Mark. Rajid and Moika's stationary trapeze work was exceptional and most of my acrobatics I'd learned from them. We all danced a little bit, then Jerry and Mark paired off to do strength poses while Rajid walked around with Moika draped over and under his shoulders. Tess grabbed me and bent me in half. I was the rag doll and Tess posed me however she wanted.

The hooting and clapping was definitely more soprano than I could ever recall. Tess had been right—our routine was approved by the ladies. When Tess straddled me to grab my ankles and pull them over my head I realized that my crotch was pointed at the room. I had a momentary panic that the fact that I was wet (again) would show, but then Tess quickly rolled me over. Just as well because my nipples were hard and really—I might want to get to know some of these women up close, but I didn't want them *all* to know that much about me.

I tackled Tess and put her through her stretches. Standing, she had one foot on the floor while I held the other pointed directly at the ceiling. My back was to the rest of the staff and the LOVE women were raising a riot. I couldn't help myself. I looked down at Tess's torso and gave the audience an appreciative wink.

After the howling abated I heard Tess ask furiously, "What did you do?"

We joined the other staffers in line, finished with a few seconds of line dancing, then bounded off the stage, the quintessence of energy. The "pros" were already in the bar, I was sure.

"I didn't do anything," I told Tess. "Except maybe make it clear that you are one beautiful woman."

Tess regarded me open-mouthed. "Why did you do that? Trying to get me a date?"

"No, I, not at all. I thought—I was just giving them what they wanted."

Tess gave me the strangest look, pissed off, flattered and flabbergasted all in one. "I don't need help getting dates, Brandy."

"I know that."

"Sometimes I think you need glasses."

"What does that mean?"

We paused at the door to the bar. It was our habit after introductions to grab a drink and mingle. It increased turnout and Club Sandzibel customer surveys reported that people who worked out were more likely to return for more vacations. Besides, it was more fun to lead classes of ten than two.

A woman I'd noticed at the pool earlier paused next to Tess. Ignoring me completely, she said, "Are we still on for that drink?"

Tess then did what I'd seen her do many times—but never before with a woman. She stepped a little closer, pushed her hair over her shoulder and gave the woman a slow blink that said yes was a possibility if the rest of the evening went well.

And then Tess went into the bar with the bleached-blonde tart!

When Tess went with some guy I watched for a bit, to make

sure he seemed okay. I always told her to be safe. If I was the least bit concerned, I'd stop for a word or two, and give the guy the "eye." That was the look that said Tess had a friend who would remember everything about him and wasn't afraid to make shit up to the cops if it would put his sorry ass in jail. I might be small, but from time to time I have been told I am scary.

Tess was sitting down with this . . . this . . . slut of a dyke, and Tess didn't even know what dykes are like. She was defenseless in the dyke dating pool. She didn't know the U-Haul syndrome, for starters. What was she thinking?

What happened to guys?

Part of me wanted to be happy for her if she was going to play for our team. I mean, Tess is fan-fucking-tastic in bed. But I had thought that our encounters were just a special thing between us, not that just any bimbo dyke from who knows where would get to feel the way Tess made me feel. It wasn't right.

It just wasn't right.

I stopped myself from barging in, stopped myself from asserting some sort of right. I had no rights to Tess. We were fuck buddies and friends. Not lovers. Not dating. Not—well, if we weren't any of those things, damn it, it was because Tess was straight. And I would think that if she wasn't straight anymore, if she'd decided she was bi, or whole-hog dyke, well, she'd tell *me*.

Why, she was with a guy just last . . . month? Wait, it was that Robert guy, when was he? February, had to be, so two months ago, wait—mistletoe. She'd felt okay with him because he'd snagged a piece of fake mistletoe and brought it over to kiss her, very romantic, the kind of move she liked. Mistletoe meant December.

Dumbfounded, I realized that Tess hadn't been with a guy for over four months. We'd had our first night together October 12, Columbus Day. And I would never forget that. We'd been together again on Halloween. And . . . Thanksgiving. Buddies, backrubs, that's all it meant.

And in all that time there'd been this Robert guy. I just hadn't noticed there weren't any after him. Tess had described him as a bit of a dud. And we'd been together New Year's Day in the afternoon, and fought back against all that romantic nonsense on Valentine's by having a grand time. St. Patrick's I'd worn a new green toy we were both curious to try.

I was so confused. So very confused to watch Tess flirt with this other woman like she meant it. It felt like I was losing something, like . . . Tess would never want me now. She could have any lesbian she wanted. I wasn't just competing with guys now—and really, dyke ego says there was no competition. Now I was competing with other dykes for this incredible woman.

Tess never stayed for breakfast and as I stood there, watching her tangle her fingers with the nobody from nowhere, I realized I really wanted her to stay for breakfast.

For the first time in my life I wanted to say about another woman, "She's with me."

"You look like somebody stole your lollipop."

I nearly jumped, but managed to look somewhat graceful—I hoped—when I turned to face Celine Griffin. "No, just watching out for a friend."

Celine nodded as if she understood. She looked exceedingly elegant in a pair of raw silk trousers and an open-crocheted short-sleeved sweater over a nearly sheer, spaghetti-strapped tank top. "I was just going to get a drink before heading to the show."

"What a good idea," I said. "Mind if I join you?"

"Not at all. I hoped you would."

When we passed Tess and whoever-she-was, Celine's hand

was on my hip. Tess saw us. She even gave me a little wink. Her color was high and I was pretty sure she wouldn't be knocking on my door later. Well, I wasn't going to be knocking on hers either. So there.

I didn't care if Tess saw that as I perched on a stool Celine's hips were between my spread knees. I was going to bed with Celine Griffin and I was going to enjoy it. When we left, frothy mudslides in hand, Celine's palm was in that zone between protectively guiding me with pressure on my lower back and openly cupping my ass. I caught the scent of Tess's cologne as we went by, but Tess never looked up.

Chapter Three

I'd have never said that a woman with a piano, telling jokes and imitating a cow's moo would put a roomful of dykes on the floor, but it did. The presence of children—lots of them, who knew dykes had so many kids!—kept the humor and conversation G-rated. I felt comfortable sitting next to Celine, laughing as heartily as she was. I was even able to put Tess out of my head for a while.

A few people wanted to chat with Celine after the program, so I waited, wishing I'd had a chance to change out of my workout clothes. I glimpsed Tess leaving with her date and wondered what on earth had gotten into me. And heck, what had gotten into her?

Nothing's changed, I thought. Nothing at all. You want to go to bed with Celine and you wish you were wearing the tight black minidress and cheeky panties, that's all. Instead I was in my day-in-day-out uniform of workout clothes and cross-trainers.

Well, Celine hadn't seemed to mind earlier. Maybe I could stop and change.

The matter was settled when she turned away from the small group she'd been chatting with and said, "Let's have that drink we discussed earlier, shall we?"

The speculative glances among the women behind her rankled somewhat. I hoped none of them thought I was some sort of straight celebrity junkie. I was a *dyke* celebrity junkie, and not really a celebrity junkie, no more than the average lesbian. Forget Tess and what anyone else thought. I thought Celine was hot, and she made my mouth water. It really was that simple.

"Whatever you want to pour," I said lightly, and we turned in the direction of Village Square. Celine continued across the plaza toward building A. I don't know why she didn't say anything. I was quiet because I was having a hard time swallowing.

The guests' rooms only looked spacious and orderly when they were unoccupied, so I was surprised—especially given how much luggage Celine had had—that her room was quite tidy. A towel was draped over a chair to dry and a pair of scuffs were tucked under the double bed nearest the door. The table was the only unruly zone: a closed laptop was nearly hidden by several folders and a variety of books stacked haphazardly.

A bottle of bourbon and two plastic cups—standard Club Sandzibel issue—sat on the glass-topped dresser next to a sweating ice bucket.

"This okay?" Celine untwisted the cap while I wondered if I should sit down.

"Yes, thank you. I'm sorry I didn't get to change."

"We're both wearing work clothes." She indicated her own attire with a wave of one hand. "This isn't my preferred date clothing."

Okay, we were having a date. I hadn't been sure. We'd skipped over that detail. I watched her hands move as she spoke, aware that I wanted to feel those hands caressing me with the same confidence with which she handled the ice and bourbon. "What would you rather be wearing?"

"Jeans. I know it seems cliché, but jeans, black T, and . . . a little something extra if I'm interested in a woman the way I am you."

I couldn't swallow again. The thought of what she described, and the echoes of our earlier conversation about control, left me speechless.

"Please, sit down. Have I shocked you? I know my onstage persona doesn't really say Top Who Likes to Pack Sometimes, does it?"

I struggled to find my voice as I sank into one of the two rattan chairs. She'd think I was some sort of gauche neophyte if I didn't speak. "I'm not shocked. I feel like . . . we've hit the ground at high speed, that's all. I'm not sure I can keep up."

"I have multiple speeds, even reverse." She recapped the bourbon while regarding me with a crooked smile. I realized that I was feeling as inexperienced as Paige probably had this morning. It's not like I've never played the way Celine was hinting at, but never with someone so . . . confident. And probably competent.

"I can say dildo, lube . . . " My voice gave out as other possibilities—courtesy of the Good Vibrations catalogue—crossed my mind.

"What about harness? Dental dam? Cock, plug?"

"Yes, though I've less experience with some of those." Okay, I'd never used a dental dam, and only read about butt plugs. Cock was just a word. I didn't mind it, but Tess and I usually used "toy." I shouldn't be thinking about Tess right now, anyway, and if that bleached-blonde dyke liked to be teased.

Celine handed me my bourbon on the rocks and we tipped the plastic cups in a casual toast. "Bonds, latex, candle wax?"

I took a quick swallow of the bourbon. She was watching me intently. It both reassured and rattled me. She wanted to know how far I would go, which meant she would go pretty far herself. "None of those."

She knelt in front of me, putting one hand on my thigh. "How about something simple? Blindfold?"

Part of me wanted to ask why we couldn't just fuck. Why did there need to be more than sweaty heat and eager hands? "Can we see how it goes? How we feel?"

"Of course," she said softly. She sipped her bourbon, then set the glass down. Her hand eased toward my inner thigh.

"I'm just a little startled," I admitted. "I'm usually the one who . . . you know . . . "

"Seduces?"

I smiled a little. Her cologne was wonderfully complex—a hint of something floral, but spicy with an edge of musk. "I never make the first move. But once a move is made . . . I consider my options. And I guess after that I do the seducing. But most of my opportunities are with straight women who are curious. So . . . I'm usually the one who says what goes because they haven't much of a clue."

"I see. So I am making you nervous."

"A little. It's just lack of practice at being . . . " I didn't quite know what to call it.

"Submissive?"

I instinctively shook my head. "I don't think of myself as submissive."

Her smile was again kind, but assessing, as if I was providing her with more and more information and she would soon know exactly what I would be comfortable with. "It means different things to different women. Not submissive, then, but . . . willing to receive? Accept?"

I could hardly breathe again. Her fingers on my thigh curled slightly, as if taking possession of my skin. "Yes, very willing."

Her eyes were nearly closed when she said, "You're making my head spin. I very much want to take you to bed and find out what will make you scream."

"I'm not saying no to that." I hoped I somehow looked sexy. I wasn't sure anymore. I had another swallow of bourbon. "I don't think it's going to take much effort."

"Not for the first, but we'll try for more, shall we?"

I hadn't known I could more than once until Tess. I cracked a smile. "Yes, please."

Both of her hands were on my thighs, edging them open. "I really want to fuck you right now."

I moaned and she heard me.

"I like women. I like the way they feel, the way they smell, the way they come. I like fucking women." She leaned between my parting thighs. "And I like to get fucked by women, Brandy. How does that sound?"

I was much more at ease, though I couldn't tell if that was her sincerity or my rapidly escalating endorphins. "That sounds perfect."

Her hands slid under my hips, pulling me to the edge of the chair. Without hesitation of any kind, she lowered her head to the crotch of my tight workout shorts. I moaned loud and long at the feel of her teeth biting through the fabric.

As wet as I was the shorts fit like a second skin. Her tongue quickly created a furrow between my swollen lips and I tipped up to meet her.

She surged against me and the chair threatened to go over backward. Grappling for balance, she grasped my forearms and the arms of the chair, holding me in place.

Her mouth felt wonderful on me. It had been a very long time since I'd felt this. Tess didn't—she had offered, and I'd said no. It was somehow more intimate, more awkward. Maybe because she wasn't gay and besides, we did care about safe sex and I didn't think I could ask her to do that for me through some sort of cling plastic wrap. It could have been a double yuck for her, I mean, it's just not what most people think of when they're glad they've got Glad. I had often wanted to taste Tess as well, but she had been with guys recently—at least I had assumed so—and at the moment I really, really wanted to feel Celine's tongue on me and I had no idea why I was thinking about Tess.

Celine sat back after a few minutes of delicious contact. My legs were trembling and she looked flushed, hungry even. "I could do that for hours, I think."

I took advantage of the moment to strip off my socks and shoes.

She grinned and said, "Don't stop there."

Feeling more confident by the minute, I sat up to peel off my Club Sandzibel tank top. As it cleared my head I felt her mouth biting my breasts through my sport bra. I cupped the back of her head and arched my back. Her hands went to the straps and she pulled them down my arms until the fabric slipped just below my nipples, framing them for her lips.

She sat back again, just looking. "You are incredibly sexy."

"So are you," I answered. It wasn't original, but I meant it. She hadn't removed a stitch of clothing, but her confidence and desire was palpable.

"Brandy, I want to . . . I'd like to arrange a few things so we don't have to stop later. I didn't think the moment I got close to you I'd want to shove my face into your cunt."

I gasped. I loved the way such raw words sounded in her sultry voice. "Can I help?"

"What I really want you to do is stay here." Her hands went under my ass and I realized she was gripping my shorts, pulling them down. "Stay here like this. Waiting for me."

She grabbed the towel from the other chair and pushed it under me once the shorts were gone. I spread my legs and she was the one who gasped then.

"Yes, just like that. Will you stay like this, too?" She briefly circled my wrists and the arm of the chair with her hands, mimicking where ties might go. My nipples hardened in response. "Waiting for me?"

I nodded. With my bra pulled down below my breasts, my arms were somewhat caught to my sides. I was glad of the towel because I was dripping.

Over the pounding of my heart I heard a suitcase being opened and other rustling noises. The rattan chair back wasn't that comfortable for resting my head, but I did lean back to relax, closing my eyes as well. The moment they were closed I could see Tess, looking down at me. Looking at my exposed places, puffed and wet, the way she had the first night we were together, after I'd lain exhausted and panting in her arms for a few minutes.

"I hadn't realized it was so beautiful," she'd said, rolling me over so she could look between my legs. "Incredibly beautiful."

I had pulled my wits together, still stunned to have discovered I could come more than once, and twined my fingers in her hair. Remembering what she had said about her needs on a night like that one, I'd said with more boldness than I'd thought possible for me, "I want to look at yours now. And then I want to fuck yours for the rest of the night."

The sound of Celine's footsteps brought me back to the moment and I slowly opened my eyes. She'd switched off most of the lights and the bedclothes had been turned back. Several more towels were stacked on the floor next to the nightstand. I saw all that in the instant before Celine herself took my breath away.

She'd removed the crochet pullover and her dark breasts

were all the more visible through the sheer tank top. Equally sheer boxer shorts didn't hide the harness and toy. I know when I wore mine I sometimes felt gawky, and not quite sure how to stand or where to put my hands. She looked comfortable and well aware that her appearance was sexy as hell. At that point the thought of feeling her inside me left me lightheaded.

"You look incredible," she said softly. "Waiting for me. Waiting for me to fuck you."

I could only nod. Holding back a whimper took the rest of my energy. I watched her take a pillow from the bed and set it on the cool tile floor in front of the chair. She knelt slowly, saying with a little smile, "I'm going to be here a while."

She caught my forearms again in her grip and stared at my small, hard nipples peeking over the top of my bra. Her gaze was so hot that I felt them swelling in response. She smiled, then quickly captured one between her lips.

Pressing hard with her mouth, she lifted my nipple slightly, then engulfed my breast completely. It was possessive and eager. She was going to devour me and after so many Paiges I was dying to be somebody's appetizer, entrée and dessert.

The intensity of her mouth on my breast made my pulse race. I moaned and didn't care that she could hear me. There was something about the way she'd asked what I liked, what I was comfortable with, that made me willing to let her push my boundaries. I didn't think of myself as submissive, but right then I was willing to give it a try as long as she didn't stop.

She was biting my nipple hard enough to make me gasp, but not so hard that it hurt. It was a fine line and the only time she went over it my reflexive flinch brought her head up.

"I'm sorry, that was too hard, wasn't it?" She cupped my nipple protectively, soothing it as she gazed into my face.

"It's okay now," I whispered.

"I'll be more careful with you." Her warm tongue brushed

lightly over my collarbone. "I don't want you to be anything but what you are."

"Me, too," I said weakly. "I mean—be what you are and I'll try to keep up."

"And what am I?"

I didn't know how to answer. My brain wasn't in operating condition. I could think of nothing clever or flattering. Only the truth came to mind. "The woman who is going to fuck me senseless."

She practically purred as she brought my hips to the edge of the chair. "This is what we both want now, isn't it?"

"Yes," I hissed. "Please."

She stood for a moment, her hips at my eye level. The shorts were so sheer that I could tell the toy was a deep purple, and thick. Thicker, perhaps, than I had felt before, but it wasn't too long for me.

I'd worn a harness myself, and with a shiver I recalled Tess's reaction when I'd had her watch me put it on. I'd been fucked with toys, but nearly always held in my lover's or my own hand. It wasn't that I didn't want to be fucked by strap-ons, it just seemed like most of my chosen bedmates preferred harness-free play. Celine was different from most of the women I'd been with, and at that moment I was pleased about that.

"Why don't you take it out?"

I was trembling as I sat up. I traced the outline of her toy with my hand and I knew that the way I was feeling it would have no trouble going inside me, and that was what I wanted. Hoarsely, I said, "Fuck me with this."

"That's exactly what I'm going to do."

Abruptly I realized that Celine was teasing me. It was just different than I was used to. All the talk about what she would do, what I liked—it was making me anticipate all of the sensations that would eventually wash over me. I was as breathless as

I'd been that first time—and every subsequent time—with Tess. Nervous, but breathless. I thought of that awkward moment when I'd shown Tess my favorite toy—I'd been shy, turned on, far from confident.

I wrapped my hand around Celine's dildo and pulled her slowly on top of me. The chair creaked as it took the weight of both of us. Aware that I was giving a kind of surrender I'd not experienced before, I said, "Tonight I think you can fuck me any way you want."

"I'm glad you like sex," she whispered.

Celine's toy brushed my clit and my whole body clenched. In my head I heard Tess whispering the same thing in my ear, "I'm glad you like sex."

"Why wouldn't I?" I said it to Celine just as I'd said it to Tess.

"Try being with some guy who wants to do it like animals, but disses you in the morning for liking it too much," Tess had said. She'd let me roll her onto her back, then sexily spread her legs so I could look at her cunt. I'd never seen one that wasn't beautiful, but hers seemed lusciously so. "I like sex, Brandy, and tonight I need to drown in it."

Celine was saying, "Haven't you ever been with a woman who wants to do it like animals, but in the morning is ashamed of her own ferocity?"

"I'm not ashamed," I told Celine. "I like sex, and I want you to fuck me." The anticipation of her cock sliding into me was so fierce that my vision swam with stars. I cupped her jaw with one hand and said fiercely, "I want to fuck you, too, however you want it. I want to feel you, too."

"We'll get there." Muscles rippled along her arms as she lowered herself onto me. "When you can't take any more."

I felt her fingers open me and I moaned and lifted my hips to her.

"Relax," she murmured. "Relax . . . we'll get to tight and hard. But right now just relax."

It wasn't just a toy any longer, not as it went into me. It seemed an extension of her passion and I could see her eyes responding to my gasping moan. It was a part of her, her toy, her cock, and she had put it on for me. Her smile was almost feral, and yes, we were going to fuck like animals and love every minute.

"Oh, yes," she breathed. "That feels so very good."

I gripped her hips with my knees, giving her the best angle. She was fully inside me in moments and we paused to breathe together, then she was out of me and in again.

I yelped and grabbed her shoulders. "God, yes!"

We found a rhythm right away. She moved in me with sharp, quick strokes while I rose to meet her. Her cock was wider than I was used to and it felt wonderful. I was wet, accepting, eager, pleading for more, and all the while watching her face and her pleasure as friction heated our skin.

The chair gave an abrupt, alarming creak and she scrambled to her feet. My back, I realized, was not happy with the position. We gave each other "should have known better" smiles and moved to the bed. I was about to sink onto my back again when she caught me in her arms from behind. I could feel her cock against my ass.

"I want you to really feel this." Her hands went to my breasts, cupping and weighing. Then her fingertips caught each nipple with a sharp tug. I groaned, felt my pussy get impossibly more wet, then I was bending for her as she slid into me from behind.

I felt more full than I ever had before and her hands on my back, holding me in place, just made me hotter. I was on my tip-toes, and she began to really move. Clinging to the bed, I groaned out "yes" to every stroke. I needed to be taken care of more than I had been letting myself feel. Pleasure, more pleasure. I was grateful for Celine's power and confidence but I also recognized that she could only give that to someone who could take it.

I could take it. I stayed with her, holding off my climax for a long, long time. She flipped me over and we inched across the bed together, hips moving in rhythm. She paused only to add more lube, which felt cool on my overheated flesh. I was getting to the point of losing control when she clamped her hands on my shoulders and held me down.

"We're just getting started," she grunted in my ear. "Come if you need to and we'll just keep going."

Her teeth against my neck triggered a hard contraction, then I was shaking under her, convulsing so hard I nearly broke her grip. My insides were cramping from hyperstimulation while my clit throbbed with pulse after pulse of pleasure. I might have cried, might have gone to sleep, but she was off of me before I stopped groaning, and her slippery hand was stroking my swollen, aching lips.

Fingers slid inside of me. I thought for a moment that my cunt had been too fucked to feel it, then she pressed firmly on my G-spot.

"Holy Christ! Don't stop—"

"I'm not going to stop."

She circled it, rubbed it, lubed her fingers again and went back to massaging me. Every time she pressed in just the right way my legs went completely limp. I tensed, clamping down on her hand.

"No, honey, loosen up. Let me do this and it will feel wonderful. Relax and let me fuck you."

Tears started in my eyes and my mouth was watering.

"Oh, you are getting so wet," Celine cooed in my ear. "You're going to come again, aren't you?"

I nodded frantically. Her fingers were unbelievably expert. I felt open, exposed. She saw what I needed and gave that to me. I suddenly felt like I couldn't let her see me this way. She was a stranger, and a powerful one. She worked my body better than I did and the responsive flutters I could feel building in my cunt were starting to scare me.

"No, no," she whispered. "Don't get tense. Stay open. Let me in. Nothing will hurt, it's just going to feel so good. Just like this. This is all we're going to do until you want to let go."

I grappled for her shoulders, weakly trying to hold on. There were no muscles in my body. I'd become all pussy, all need, and that frightened me. I told myself not to be afraid. Not to resist. I liked sex. It was okay to say yes, okay to come, okay to . . . okay to . . . cry out, to arch up, to feel waves of contractions so hard and close together that I couldn't breathe.

Celine moaned. "Dear heaven, yes, let it go, baby . . . oh, yes."

The sensation was a mix of opposites. I felt full and empty, wet and dry. Open for anything and so tight I couldn't believe her fingers could stay inside me. I wanted to cry and laugh, beg her to stop and plead with her to do more.

Then it was over and I was limp in her arms.

"Wow," Celine murmured some time later. "That was unbelievable."

Her face was all smiles with a definite helping of preening. I blushed slightly, feeling unbelievably shy and unattractive. I was covered in sweat, lying in a puddle and the hair on the back of my head had no doubt ratted into a snarled mess. "Mm-hmm."

"Oh, now don't get embarrassed. That felt good, didn't it?"

"Yes," I said, still feeling sheepish. "I don't think I've quite ever . . . done that. Not like that." I thought of Tess, who knew exactly how I liked a handheld dildo to feel, but hadn't ever tried to fuck me with her hand. I wondered why not—was going inside me with her fingers, that deep and that hard, outside of what she was willing to do for a . . . friend? Or had I not told her that I could like that? "I'm finding it hard to catch my breath."

"That's okay. Just breathe. Cool down."

"Who's the trainer here?" I gave her what I hoped was a flirtatious look that implied at any moment I'd have the strength and drive to do her the way she'd done me. But it was going to take longer than a minute.

"Right now, I am," she answered with a grin.

"You're pleased with yourself, aren't you?"

"Damn right. Here," she handed me a towel. "You roll over to that side of the bed and I'll get rid of the wet ones."

Good lord, I was covered, I realized. Covered with the same salty, sticky residue that had coated Paige's legs this morning, but Paige hadn't been a shaking, hopeless, shellshocked mess afterward. Celine was the best fuck I'd ever had.

That thought brought Tess to mind again. Tess didn't count. Tess and I didn't . . . We didn't fuck the same way. She wasn't a lesbian and we were just friends—it felt different with her. I wondered, then, if she was with that bleached blonde, getting fucked, feeling the same kind of stunned completion I was feeling? Could she with someone else?

Was I satisfied? My body was limp, so why was my head spinning like something wasn't yet done? Celine wasn't done, that was true, but this confusion wasn't about Celine. It was something in my head I couldn't figure out. A surprise, something unknown, but I didn't know what it was.

Celine settled behind me and nuzzled my neck. "How are you feeling?"

"Totally fucked," I admitted. I barely had the energy to

speak. The sex energy was fading, and the subsequent rush of satisfaction endorphins made me want to sleep.

"Good. That was my goal."

"You may have done your job too well. I could sleep all night, right now."

Her hand brushed the side of my breast, and she slowly, deliberately took hold of my still sensitized nipples. I gasped at how good it felt. "You could, but I don't think you will."

A different kind of arousal swelled through me. My dyke ego wanted to have something to strut about, too. I reached back with my hand, finding her thighs, and without hesitation pushed it between them.

She was steaming hot, slippery, and she moaned. She moaned low and long, and her legs opened for me.

My back still to her, I said huskily, "You liked fucking me, didn't you?"

"Yes." It sounded like she was gritting her teeth.

Grinning with anticipation, two of my fingers were quickly slicked with her copious juices. She slid her cunt along my fingers, gliding over them. She felt very good, swollen and thick.

Without removing my hand I slowly rolled over to face her. She was panting and not hiding it.

Slowly, so I understood every word, she said, "I like to be fucked hard. And I like it to be fast."

"Let's take care of this and have some fun, then." I used my free hand to undo one buckle of her harness. After a moment, she undid the other. Two snaps later I tossed the harness and toy onto the room's other double bed.

I firmly believe that all women are beautiful naked, and Celine was all that and more. The dark curves of her hips against the white sheets tempted me to massage them and I knelt to kiss her stomach, her chest, then her small, firm breasts.

I was settling in to tease her nipples when she shoved my hand between her legs.

"Fuck me, hard and fast."

"Yes," I murmured. "Let's do that." I gave her nipples a longing look. I'd have liked to linger a while. But it was obvious that she was ready to move to higher pleasures.

I slicked the back of my hand with lube and her wetness and sank two fingers inside her. It wasn't enough. With a thrill running down my back, I went into her with four and brought my thumb down on her clit. My fingers were gloriously, deliciously wet.

She hissed in response and her hips met my first hard, deep thrust. "Like that! Don't stop."

My knuckles massaged the trembling walls of her cunt and I reveled in the way she tightened in response. Her cunt was tight and wet around my hand and we groaned together when a contraction seized her. She was close. I couldn't feel her G-spot but it hardly seemed to matter. She caught my waist with her legs, crushing me to her, and I felt wave after wave of rippling muscles inside her cunt, loving my hand back.

Panting over her, I waited for her to slump before I took my hand away. Her low, easy laugh had me crawling into her arms.

"Would it be rude of me to ask where you learned to fuck like that?" I traced a lazy circle on her chest then settled my head against her again. We'd been cuddling for a half-hour, just talking off and on about whatever topic came to mind. Sex, primarily.

"Not rude . . . I can't really say I've had lessons. I've just always done what I preferred and practice always helps."

"Reps and sets, eh?"

"Something like that. It's a good workout, wouldn't you say?"

"You need to remember to stretch out before and after."

She did stretch, her long body going rigid, then limp against me. "Thank you, O, physical trainer. You must get lots of practice."

"Of one kind or another. Straight women seem to find me attractive." I thought of Tess yet again. I was so confused. I needed to talk to her, obviously.

"I imagine that has its limitations."

"Yes, it does. I got tired of being that kind of physical trainer. There was a girl in college. Madeline. I should have learned it all then, I think."

"Broke your heart?"

"Yeah." I hadn't thought about Madeline in a while. "She told me she was straight, but she made love like a dyke. And wanted me. And liked sex with me. I thought she loved me too."

"And you were thinking about forever?"

In the dim light I couldn't tell if she found that unsophisticated. "I was. I've given up on that. Forever isn't real."

"I used to think that. Now, I think it's just a lucky few and I'm not one of them."

"Me, neither." The endorphins were starting to fade and I felt vaguely depressed. "My parents are still married, but it's not the kind of forever I want, with a tankard of Trapped for dinner chased by a bowl of Bitter for breakfast. Of course, working here I don't get much chance to meet anyone."

"Why don't you move someplace with more dykes? You'd have a fun time."

"I suppose in time I might go for a teaching credential and see if I can get a college or high school job. But this one seemed pretty nice when I took it. Not a lot of responsibilities."

"You're just putting off growing up. It's inevitable."

Frowning, I said, "If growing up means standing in one place, I'd rather not."

"Ignore me, then." Her voice had softened. "Hell, it's rare enough in this world to make your living at what makes you happy. Go for it. Believe in it."

"Thanks." I kissed her shoulder. "My best friend and I occasionally get off this island and into Fort Myers, even Tampa, but the best I can hope for is the riot girls' bar. I've been saving for a trip down to Key West just to hang in a gay-friendly place. But then LOVE came to visit my world."

"I don't usually do this, Brandy. I mean, I do. I like women and I love nights like tonight. But I don't usually find someone on the first night. I live in Cheyenne near my folks when I'm not traveling. Doing tours is just moving from town to town. I tell jokes to audiences full of dykes and they all go home and I go to the motel. Then I get to these vacations and there's this magic in the air, all these lesbians filling up the ship or the resort and I get . . . really . . . "

I cupped her breast and was delighted to feel her nipple harden under my palm. "I know. Something hit me like a sledgehammer the moment LOVE arrived."

"There was this one night in Alaska, seven hundred women on the ship. The inland passage was like glass, the moon was full, and it was actually mild out. After the night show the place emptied. Nobody went to the disco, nobody in the casino. Everyone was out on deck or in their cabin. The captain asked me if it was some sort of special night for the ladies, like solstice or something. I just looked at him and said of course it was special, they were all in love and free to feel it. He just laughed and admitted he was used to a more geriatric crowd, and he'd set the stabilizers for a lot of rocking motion."

"And even though it was smooth out, did anyone get seasick?"

She laughed. "That's a good punch line. I'm gonna steal it."

"Okay." Her nipple had stayed hard and I slowly circled it with my fingertip. I wondered if I'd hear my words in some future routine. It was one way to be memorable, I supposed.

"Nights like that I believe more in forever. But mostly, I don't think it's for me." She sighed. "Of course I can't decide if I've made up my mind it's not for me because it's never going to happen, or if it's that I'm really not a forever kind of gal. You, at least, have a couple of decades until you get to where I am."

I sighed. "And I'll never know, just going to bed with straight women who really like the sex until it's time to touch me. At least in college there were lesbians. I was a phys. ed. major, and believe me, there were lots of lesbians."

"Where'd you go to school?" Her hand played slowly along my hip.

"U.C. Santa Barbara. I played golf and soccer. I was nearly an alternate for Women's World Cup."

"Wow." Her hand cupped my ass. "I can feel all that."

I leaned over her to lick her tantalizing nipple. "You can feel it all you want tonight."

"Just tonight?"

"I'm here all week." I slipped my hand between her thighs, just to see if I was right about the slight movement of her hips. Why yes, I was right.

She opened her legs and we smiled at each other in the low light. I wouldn't be so foolish as to fall in love with those yellow-ringed eyes and that supple, powerful but yielding body, but I could hold a serious case of lust for quite a while.

My day ended much better than it began, with the two of us moaning long into the night. As I finally drifted to sleep, under the weight of Celine's arm, I wondered what Tess was doing, and if she was happy. I wanted her to be happy. I wanted her to know . . . I wanted her to . . .

Chapter Four

Too soon my body's internal clock woke me. I didn't have to look to know it was after eight. Morning Stretch was in less than an hour. I needed to shower and get some water and protein in my body before then.

I slipped out from under Celine's arm and didn't mind in the least that parts of me were sore. I obviously hadn't stretched sufficiently beforehand, and the workout had been intense. I paused long enough in the bathroom to scrawl "See you later?" on a notepad, which I left propped over the bathroom faucet so Celine would definitely see it.

Smiling, I made my way to my quarters, trudging up the stairs with a goofy look on my face. I knew it was goofy because I ran smack into Tess, and her smile was exactly the way I felt, and it looked goofy.

We stared idiotically at each other. Without thinking better of it, I said, "So when did you give up on men? Or have you?"

Tess shrugged. "Men are men. I just haven't wanted one in a while. I got tired of never feeling safe. And never having anything to talk about. And not getting what I needed nine times out of ten."

I hesitated. "Was it because of . . . "

"Geez, Brandy, are you angling for another toaster oven?" Her eyes flashed. "Fine, you get the prize. List me as a reference."

"That wasn't what I meant." But I was talking to Tess's back.

"I need to get ready for Body Pump," she said over her shoulder.

She had an hour more than I did to get ready for her day. "That really wasn't what I meant. Tess?"

Her door closed and I stood there for a few minutes, trying to figure out why the conversation had derailed. I finally decided that coming out was never easy, and Tess was probably just as surprised by it as anyone would be. I'd give her a lot of time and space and eventually my best friend would talk to me about it. I could wait until lunch, even.

Sundays most of the guests sleep in, but there is usually a half-dozen core group of devotees that rises with the sun, jogs on the beach, makes protein shakes for breakfast and then turns up for Morning Stretch. Sunday is the first full day on the premises and the goal is for every guest to take part in at least one activity. We want them to join the Club Sandzibel family, yes we do.

Munching the last of my banana and yogurt, my footsteps slowed as I reached the deck where guests were already gathering. There must have been twenty-five women there, slipping out of their Kangaroos and Tevas, shinnying off beach covers or mopping their brows—and chests—with towels from the fitness center.

Wow. I was about to have at least two dozen dykes on their backs, panting for me. Okay, panting with me, but a girl could fantasize, couldn't she?

I didn't really have to work at fantasizing. Pelvises raised and lowered, legs spread and crossed, and arms reached out in supplication at my merest command. I was a Nathor, Goddess with Upraised Arms, and they were my acolytes, eager to please my every whim.

Wow. This was pretty cool. I felt as if sunlight sparkled in my blood even though I'd been up late. I could have given them all a workout for the entire morning, but Tess showed up to urge everyone to Body Pump, and when nearly everyone went, I tagged along.

Now Tess was Nathor with a barbell and we were all in heaven. I was at the back of the class, and if the landscape had been sublime with all of those lovely women on their backs, it was even better when they all touched their toes.

I guess I was no better than a guy, ogling all that female flesh, but at least I didn't think I owned it or had a right to it. I was just enjoying the view, in all its variety. There was no end to the diversity of women's butts.

Tess caught me at it, and I blushed.

Looking wicked, she said, "Brandy, maybe you'd like to help me go through the arms portion."

Well, damn. I nearly pouted, but as I reached the front of the class and regarded the rows of muscle-shirted, tank-topped and sport-braed figures it was all okay.

Maybe someday I would grow up, but I hoped never to be so closed up that I couldn't look at women and feel the magic of the female working in my blood.

"You were showing off," Tess accused me when the class was over.

"Was not." I put down the twenty-pound weights I'd been

using for curls, carefully hiding the wince as my muscles went into spasm. I had no idea what Tess meant.

"You won't be able to raise your arms tomorrow," she predicted.

I couldn't raise my arms right then, but I wasn't telling her that. "First time I've ever seen you use a fifteen," I pointed out.

"I was due to step up."

"Right." I saw the bleached blonde from last night approaching, looking very cool and calm. Studly. Smug. No way, I thought. Even though the very first time with Tess she had said I'd taken care of her better than she ever had been before, it still had taken several times to get scratches-down-the-back perfect.

Bleachie had no right to look so insufferable. Good sex was hard work, and Tess and I had practiced and we were . . . not a couple, okay. But we were *something*. What if Tess was looking at the future, too, the way thoughts of it had been plaguing me for the last twenty-four hours? What if she was thinking about forever. Well, she wouldn't find it with some one-week wonder. I don't think she realized that dykes were the same as straight women when it came to vacation conditions—no relationship would last past Saturday.

Tess was already saying hello, flipping her hair. While I stood wondering how to cut Bleachie off at the pass the two of them were falling into step toward the guest rooms in building B. Obviously, Tess had plans for her hour's break.

It didn't seem right that Tess was getting more, given that she was the newbie, while I was wondering if I'd see Celine again before nightfall. I was the one with experience dating dykes. Okay, maybe not so much lately. But wouldn't it be just *perfect* if Tess went and fell in love with the first dyke she went to bed with?

I stomped back to my quarters and shoved Celine's framed magazine cover in a drawer. Really, Tess had had no right to imply I was being childish by showing off with the weights. Holding back a groan at the ache in my arms, I did some basic cleaning up in case I needed to invite somebody in for some reason. My hour's break was nearly up before I had finished the dishes and sweeping. The laundry pile was just going to have to wait. I had to hotfoot it to KidZone to relieve Rhea and her staffers in time.

There was no sign of Tess, of course. She was busy getting laid, I was sure. Rajid and I showed a group of five-year-olds how to do somersaults. I bandaged a scraped knee—including filling out the incident report—and left an hour later not terribly improved in mood. Tess was in the pool by then, for another round of pool games. Her skin looked flushed and alive and her eyes were glowing with vitality. She looked like she'd had a wonderful morning. Which was just *perfect*.

It was even more perfect when she clambered out of the pool and I got a look at her back where the swimsuit usually snugged up. Scratches, four on each side, which meant Bleachie had had a good time too.

Time for lunch. I snagged the last three slices of chocolate bread and damn me if I was going to share.

With a little time before the afternoon Body Pump, I took my water bottle down to the beach. I had twenty minutes to soak up the peaceful sounds of the surf, and the turmoil I felt in my head was giving me no peace.

It was the scratches. That meant that Tess had been on top and Bleachie had been feeling *really* good. I had scratched Tess's back, just that way, when what she was doing to me felt so good I couldn't help it. I wasn't the only one, either. I shivered when I remembered Tess's nails going down my back that first night, not to mention several nights since. But that first night she'd marked me the deepest.

I'd felt a little shy when I'd put on the harness. Her toy was larger than I was used to wearing, and switching the ring to hold it and then readjusting all the buckles had, I thought, diminished some of the magic with tedious technical details. When I was finally set to go, Tess sat back on the bed and openly looked me over.

I blushed. I wasn't used to someone assessing me while I was wearing the thing. I'd feel more comfortable when I was fucking her. I blushed harder as my mind gave me an anticipatory vision of what that would be like, to be on top of Tess and feel her body rise and fall because of what I was doing to her.

"I can't believe we're doing this." Her voice was low and soft.

"I can't believe what you've already done to me."

"I loved it." She slowly brought her fingertips to my nipples, which responded almost instantly to her touch. "Touching you was . . . not what I expected. I didn't think it could feel so good."

I cupped her hands against my breasts. "You have great hands. They feel wonderful. But if you don't stop, we'll never get to the fun for you."

She gave me a nervous glance. "Are you sure? I mean, that you want to do this?"

My voice raspy with desire, I said, "I'm going to enjoy it. Are you sure?"

"Yes, please," she said quickly. "Everything I felt before, I feel it ten times more now."

I thought about the hours she had spent making every nerve in my body come to life, and I thought how good her skin had felt against mine. Gently, looking directly into her eyes, I pushed her back on the bed. She melted under me, making me feel like a sun goddess.

I kissed her jaw, then nuzzled her ear. "Talk to me, tell me what will feel good."

"Right now," she said hoarsely, "I want that thing inside me."

Resting my weight on one elbow, I reached between her legs.

My fingers were swimming in her hot, thick wetness. Slippery and soft, her lips were the most sensuous thing I'd touched in ages.

She mewled softly. "Please, I can't take being teased."

"I'm not teasing," I said. "I'm going to fuck you, Tess, the way you want it." I sank two fingers in her, then brought them up to circle her clit. "I'm opening you up so you can take it. So it can slide in so easy. So . . . oh, that feels *good*, doesn't it?"

Her legs had wrapped around my thighs as I rubbed her hardening clit. She let out a startled cry and I realized she was climaxing, everything rigid and tight against my hand. I hurriedly wet the toy with my slick hand and pushed the head against her opening.

She was gasping for breath, and I saw tears in her eyes. "Please, Brandy, please, fuck me—take me—just have me— *please*."

I'd never used something so big and I was afraid I'd hurt her, but she knew what she wanted and I pushed in. She was crying and moaning and I started to move, faster and faster. Her chest was flushed with need. Her eyes glimmered with tears.

"I'm sorry." She panted for breath. "Sorry, you have to fuck me so hard—"

I shushed her. "You are so hot and so sexy, Tess. I love doing this. I'm just getting started."

"Don't stop." She grasped my shoulders with her hands. The sound of our bodies meeting was delicious. The level of her abandon was so high I could only marvel. I loved women, and she felt simply fabulous under me. Like nothing I'd ever felt before.

Her eyes were tightly shut and her nails were starting to dig into my shoulders. "Please don't stop, please don't come yet, please—"

"Look at me, Tess." I slid in so deep she gasped and her eyes

76

flew open. "I'm a woman, and I can fuck you all night. All day. I won't stop, and I will love every second of it."

"Brandy." She wrapped her arms around me tight, pulling me down until all my weight was on her. Our hips were grinding together. I stayed with her movements, even as they became more and more exaggerated. I don't know how long we stayed that way, but, like Tess, I was feeling hungrier and hungrier with each passing minute. I wanted to do this all night, slide in and out of her, feel her dancing under me.

She was close again, close for a long time, then she groaned and I felt her body swell. Very close now. I could feel it in the tautness of her breasts and the grip of her muscles on the toy.

"Until you're done. I won't leave you feeling like this. You feel so good under me, so sweet and hot. God, it's wonderful to fuck this way."

She cried out and her fists came down on my back and we writhed together, arms and legs locked, straining so hard against each other I thought one of us would surely break.

A few minutes later, after Tess had blown her nose and had a drink of water, she managed a weak smile. "That was . . . closer than I've ever gotten. Thank you."

I was a little puzzled because earlier it had sounded like she didn't stop after two, especially when the first one was pleasing, but small. I wondered if I'd done something wrong, or if she thought if we did more I wouldn't take care of her. I nearly said something inane, but her nipples gave her away. Still hard, they told me she was turned on.

"We're not done." I rubbed the underside of one nipple with my fingertip. "I want to fuck you again. And again."

A shudder traveled the length of her body and her arms were dusted in goose flesh. "You don't have to . . . I've already . . . "

"You think I'm tired? That I'm just doing you a favor?"

She didn't answer, but her eyes were clouded with doubt.

"I'm not tired, Tess. And believe me, the pleasure is all mine." I took her hand and placed it on my soaked crotch. "Feel that? I love pleasing you."

"Oh . . . " she breathed. Her fingers curled into my wet cunt. "You feel good, I didn't know. I could touch you all night—"

"No, right now we're taking care of you," I said firmly.

Tess stared at me with eyes that seemed frightened, not of me, but of herself. "It's just one night," she finally said, in a broken voice. "I'm not like this all the time, I promise."

"Even if you were, what's wrong with that? What's wrong with feeling really good?"

"You're not just a—a dildo to me." She pointed at the heavy toy. "I—"

"And you weren't either, Tess. We're friends, remember? I care about how you feel. And right now, I think we're talking too much. I want to fuck you again."

She gasped and it was all I needed. I couldn't stop talking after that. Words I'd thought but never said bubbled out of me, about how good cold lube could feel drizzled on a hot clit, the way her nipples felt in my mouth when they hardened. I explored her body in more detail than I had even my own. Using just my hand I played in her cunt, opening, stroking, fucking, massaging the inside of her, my groans matching hers as her body responded.

With my hand covered in lube I could go deep. I was in past my knuckles with my thumb on her clit. I'd never done more than that to any woman but Tess might be open enough to take my whole hand. But it seemed like . . . like I ought to ask, and I didn't want to stop to ask, not when she was going to come for me this way.

I didn't want her to think I was going to hurt her or that I

78

wanted to hurt her. I wasn't sure I wouldn't, even with all the lube and how much it felt like she could take. I'd read about it but never thought I'd be with a woman where it seemed possible. More than possible, it seemed natural to the way Tess felt inside.

I wasn't sure I could do it, either, even though it seemed like it would be easy with her. I wasn't a macho slut, a bedroom daddy or any other Bad Girl I'd read about in books. I was just me. The more I thought about it, the more I wanted to go inside her, fill her completely. I thought she would love it, she felt so hot and open, but doing that to her seemed like something a lover would do, and I wasn't her lover. I could use on her the toy she allowed, but to fist her—she wasn't mine that way.

I turned my fingers to stroke her steadily.

"Brandy, don't stop, oh *please*."

"I won't, I won't. I'm filling you up and you are going to come on my hand." I pushed hard, spreading my fingers inside her. "All over my hand."

She seemed startled when climax hit her, as if coming this way, with only my fingers inside her, wasn't part of what she thought she needed on a night like tonight. Like the orgasm before she got tight, then astonishingly open and wet. I felt waves of contractions around my hand, then she relaxed slightly.

I looked down into her face, and found her staring up at me. She wanted to ask for more but I could tell something was holding her back. Fear I would say no or laugh? That I'd roll over and go to sleep? "Feel that?"

She nodded frantically.

"I'm getting this nice, big toy all slippery again."

A tiny whimper escaped her.

"Now I'm going to push it inside you, inside you where you want it."

"Please."

I looked down at the toy as I guided it inside her, amazed that something so thick could disappear with such ease. The sound it made opening her up again tightened my spine and we were in each other's arms again, holding tight, straining.

Her body seemed to swell when I went in and flatten when I pulled out. The effect of my every move was profound and I found myself whispering in her ear, "It feels so good, Tess, so good to be on top of you. To fuck you and feel how much you like it."

For several minutes all she could say, in a desperate, ragged voice, was, "Don't stop."

"I will take care of you," I had said, over and over, and when she came we hadn't stopped. I had slathered the toy and my hand with lube and we started all over.

Water trickling around my toes brought me back to where I was. The tide had shifted enough that a particularly energetic wave had reached my shady spot. I rose to dust myself free of sand and tiny shells. Hell, I was almost late to afternoon Body Pump.

Celine was there but to my own surprise, while I felt quite warm and friendly to see her, I wasn't overwhelmed with the desire to drag her off to a private place and repeat some or all of the previous night's activities. She smiled at me with a decided twinkle, but my ego wasn't bruised in the least that she was chatting flirtatiously with one of the other guests. It had been fantastic, but I had to face facts. Fantastic, but Celine wasn't Tess.

And I was a fool to let that matter.

Endorphins, as I've studied and experienced, can work for you, even if you're feeling like an idiot loser dumbshit with no more sense than a baby to go falling in love with a friend and a woman who may just be dabbling in lesbian sex. Tess would be mortified to know how I felt. Lord knows, I was pretty embarrassed.

I led the large group through lunges, lifts, balance workouts and squats, and all the while I was thinking, "You're in love with her, and you want more than you've got with her, and if she finds out it's all over."

Madeline had broken my heart, smashed it into tiny bits. She'd wanted sex with me like crazy, had loved to fuck me, go down on me, everything. And I'd loved being with her. I really had thought she wasn't straight. At a minimum, she was bi. I thought she was in love with me, the person, and that I was a woman who had some definite pluses. She left me for a law school grad with a guaranteed six-figure job at his daddy's firm. I could understand marrying for security, though it wasn't something I thought I'd ever do. What I didn't understand was her parting shot: "Besides, you're a woman. Two women can't build a future and a family. It's just a sham."

At the time, crying too hard to even answer, I hadn't really thought about what a crock of shit that was, and how much Madeline must have hated herself to think that no matter what woman she hooked up with she couldn't make it real.

Just thinking about it pissed me off all over again. I wasn't going to let Tess hurt me that way, but hell, what was I thinking? Tess and I were fuck buddies. We weren't about love and forever and wanting shit like that. We were free to do anybody we liked, and for her, that could include every guy on the premises and I wasn't supposed to care.

Except I did care. Not about guys, but about other women.

I cared about Bleachie and if she'd made Tess feel better than I had. I cared that Tess seemed angry with me about something, and I cared that I had had a fabulous night of sex but had no desire to repeat it if it wasn't with Tess.

I was supposed to be a free bird. I wanted to be. I wanted to act on my feelings, and feel love with anyone who tightened my skin and gave my heart that flutter. Celine had done that yesterday. All of these women had done that yesterday, but today I wanted Tess.

This was a revolting turn of events and as far I could tell, it was up to me to fix it. This was not Tess's problem. Maybe I was just jealous, worried about being upstaged by other dykes. I had to get over being jealous of Bleachie. Maybe I should go to bed with Bleachie. Maybe Tess and I could both go to bed with Bleachie.

My body did respond to that thought. I switched the class over to slower-paced arm lifts and realized that I had no trouble picturing me showing Bleachie how Tess liked to be touched.

But then the fantasy got fuzzy. My mind kept wanting to turn it toward Tess and me sending Bleachie out for ice or pizza or something, and Bleachie being gone for a long time, like, oh, forever, while Tess and I made love and just plain fucked ourselves silly for hours, days, years. Instead, reality intruded. Bleachie learned all my moves and then it was me who went out for ice and found the door locked on my return.

She's a free woman, I told myself. Try to capture her and she'll leave you. If she figures you want more than holiday fucks and midnight brownies, she'll leave you. If you act jealous, she'll leave you. If you do anything but what you've done for the last six months, she'll leave you.

I hate having to think this hard. I hate having to wonder if it's possible to get dumped by somebody who doesn't even think you're a couple.

Celine gave me a friendly wave as she walked off with her new flirting pal. I found the presence of mind to tip a pretend hat to her. My arms were screaming from using the twenty-pound weights that morning, and I stank to high heaven. It was my afternoon off, and what I really needed was a shower and a nap.

I had the shower, but sleep refused to come to bed with me, as no doubt Tess would next time I asked.

The sight of the dining room full of women, women and, for a change, more women, lifted my spirits. I treated myself to a heap of fresh strawberries and Greek salad with chicken in a light pesto.

"I remember how you like it." Marianne—in charge of soup, cheeses and bread—added extra fontina to the bowl before ladling in the French onion soup.

"If you weren't already married, I'd be on my knees begging," I told her.

She regarded me with a twinkle as she dusted a crumb from her matronly bosom. "I tell my husband I have attractive girl who wants to marry me. Know what he say? He say, bring her home, we all have fun."

"Your husband," I observed after we stopped laughing, "is a dirty old man."

If anything, she twinkled harder. "That's why I love him, yes?"

"You give me hope, Marianne." I hoisted my steaming bowl and dinner plate and realized I had enough cheese to harden my arteries on the spot. Well, maybe if they got hard my heart would as well.

Tess was probably scrambling into her Sunday evening costume. Tonight, the LOVE comedienne who'd performed last night was hosting our takeoff of the *Gong Show*. Tess's belted-out version of "What Now My Love?" usually brought the house down, especially when, during a particularly deep breath, the waist of her skirt popped open to display elaborate pantaloons that said "kick me" on the butt. This never failed to make the children howl, and the louder the kids laughed, the more the grownups did too.

My job for the show was behind the scenes—pinning costumes, drawing the curtains and rolling scenery up and down. I often thought I got off easy. The resort preferred to hire multi-talented staffers, ones who could not only do their assigned work, like reception managers and chefs, but double as entertainers. My "talent" during the interview had been a hastily contrived tumbling routine, ending with a nothing-short-of-miraculous handstand walk.

I had needed the job, and badly. My parents heartily disapproved of my chosen "mannish" major, but their disapproval of my "deviance" was infinitely more hearty. Perverts were on their own. Only in my most generous moments was I thankful they had at least—as promised to both my brother and me—paid for college. Of course my younger brother, Roger, got tuition and room and board so working wouldn't interfere with his business major, while I was tuition-only. Physical education wasn't really studying, you know.

I was on my own after that. Roger, the pig, was as big a homophobe as my parents were. I hoped they all choked on their Baltimore air. Someday I hope no longer to care anything about them.

I had walked across that damn stage on my hands, then backflipped twice, a feat I'd never equaled since. And I got the job, making a living using my college education. Mostly. It didn't pay terribly well, but I lived for free. The hours were long, six days a week, and management completely arbitrary. I would have liked a car, cell phone and broadband, but I would have hardly had time to enjoy them. And I knew that I could work just as many hours, in just as frustrating circumstances, flipping burgers for the same disposable income. In my odd hours here

I got to dig my toes in the sand. The sunshine, pool and weekly morning round of golf were all free.

Tomorrow the circus tumbling lessons began. Thursday night was the big circus show featuring all the kids who were allowed to practice on the trapeze and mats. I liked teaching them and then watching them do it with the lights and music. It beat stuffing fries into paper bags any day.

When I'd dragged myself back out of bed before dinner I decided against my usual practical workout attire. Instead I'd found a lightweight pair of black slacks and a sage green sleeveless shirt. That combination worked well with my hair, tamed with detangling spray. At the very last minute I'd clipped on simple gold earrings. I wasn't sure why I was making an effort. I wasn't trying to catch anyone's attention and Tess had seen the outfit once a week for the last two years. It might have passed for simple elegance but for the Club Sandzibel nametag, required at all but off-duty times. The tag's red background clashed with both shirt and hair, but there was nothing I could do about it.

Randall, who knew how to ruin just about any good mood, commented, "A bit dressed for a stagehand, aren't you?"

I ignored him, which was my usual policy and had so far served me well. I hoped Tess was right and he'd be shipped out soon. The club music in the general seating area was dying down and, forgetting all about me, Randall dashed onstage to introduce the evening's entertainment. The next sixty minutes were busy, but we all knew the pacing. I had the sets down in time and still managed to help Tess out of her costume after her bit.

"Thanks," she muttered as I finally got a knot out of the last tie.

"That's three that weren't right. Were you in some sort of hurry?" I didn't mean to smirk or sound curious, but I did, no getting around that.

"Something like that. Gloria tried to help, but she wasn't as good at it as you."

I nearly asked if *Gloria* was not as good at other things, but I thought better of it, just in time. Tess sped off to make a quick change for the final dance number.

After the show I filed out with everyone else. The night air was hot and sticky and I noticed most of the women were heading for their rooms. I didn't blame them. It wasn't a night to sit out by the pool. I thought about a cold drink, realized I could have one for free in my own quarters and told myself it wouldn't hurt me in the least to spend the night alone. Even if Celine wanted to do more, my body could probably use a little recovery time. Certainly my arms were still telling me about those twenty-pound weights.

"Brandy!" Celine broke away from a cluster I hadn't noticed and I paused to let her catch up to me. "Do you think we'd have any luck getting the D.J. in the disco to change the music? What do you think?"

"Can't hurt to ask," I said. "They do have to balance the tastes of the whole bar."

"There's nobody in there and I got a kind of a grunt when I asked."

Had to be Emilio, whose attitude drove me nuts. Emilio knew best what we *ought* to dance to, so of course any requests to the contrary were met with a sneer. I had told Tess that Emilio must have learned customer service at a music store for the fatally hip. Randall liked Emilio because he could get the place hopping and trays of drinks were consumed. Every week was different, though.

I flinched as we walked in the door. I like Aphex Twin as much as the next girl, but not at a volume that induced pain.

The booth was much quieter. Emilio was reading a Cuban newspaper and looking in a foul mood.

86

"They don't drink, so why should I care what they want to dance to?"

"They have to drink something, and something is better than nothing. I'll tell Trevor it's a well-known fact that dyke moms don't drink, and you did well to sell ice to the Eskimos. But they won't hang around if you don't turn the volume down so they can hear themselves talk, and pick some music they can dance to."

"What? Like the, uh, Beach-a Boys?"

"Yeah, like that. Put on 'Surfin' Safari' and suggest how good an ice-cold light beer would taste right now."

He snapped open his paper as if he was going back to reading, then he threw the paper on the floor. "Fine. Have it your way. Soon we will have nothing but the, uh, flower power crowd and we'll add prune juice to the daily special."

"They'll only be here a week, Emilio. I know you can dance their butts off the floor, too. Queue up five and offer to swing— dykes *love* queens. You'll be the belle of the ball, trust me."

He gave me a scathing look, but his hands were already flitting over the console. Moments later Lou Vega mellowed the room with "Mambo #5" and there was an audible cheer from the other side of the door. I bowed deeply to Emilio's good taste and hid my smile that he was peeking at the women. He'd be on the floor if any of them looked like they'd dance.

There was applause as I emerged from the booth, led by Celine.

"Please, please," I said, in my best Thanking the Little People manner. "No need to worship the ground I walk on."

"Thank you!" Celine was already moving in rhythm, and several couples were bouncing on their toes, evaluating the room's energy. I didn't realize Celine had moved closer until her mouth was on mine for a firm, not entirely tongue-free kiss.

"Oh!" I couldn't have sounded more gauche, so I tried to cover it by adding, "You like me, you really, really like me."

"That I do," she answered. "There's a whole group that wasn't ready to go to bed yet."

"Me, I'm about to drop," I said hastily. "I didn't sleep much last night."

"Neither did I. I'm not sure I'll sleep well tonight either." She made what I took to be a nod in the direction of one of the LOVE organizers.

"Enjoy," I said without any rancor. "I need to go talk to the bar manager." Last night had been fabulous. Maybe in a few days I'd feel differently about repeating it. Right then, all I wanted was my bed, alone.

Okay, if Tess had been there, asking me to make love to her, that would have been pretty good, too.

I made my way to the bar and told Trevor, the bar manager, that he might do well to run beer pitchers on some sort of special and get some baskets of tortilla chips into the disco.

"You think that'll work? Last night things moved okay, but tonight it was like booze was poison."

"It's too hot to sit out," I consoled. "And the ladies aren't big drinkers usually. Emilio's trying to be a good sport with the music."

Trevor gave me a considering look. "Thanks for being a go-between. Why don't you come work the bar when you're tired of sweating in the sun? You'd be good at it, and you've got a brain, which helps."

I was flattered. Trevor had a brain, too, and it was nice to be noticed.

"I'll think about it," I said noncommittally. Bed was starting to call really loudly.

The night felt heavy and smelled faintly of ozone. Thunderclouds were moving across the stars and the wind was rising. I quickened my step, expecting rain any second, and passed several slow-moving couples strolling along the path outlining the beach, holding hands. They didn't seem to care where they were or what time it was or what the weather was planning to do. They were in their own worlds and part of me wanted to scoff, but another part of me was just plain envious.

I was most of the way up my stairs when I realized that Tess was going into her place, and she wasn't alone. Bleachie— Gloria, I supposed—was with her. They were most of the way in the door, making out like crazy.

I tortured myself for a minute, watching Bleachie unbutton Tess's blouse. It started to rain and I didn't move. My mouth watered at the sight of Tess's nipples and I was suffused with heat. I wanted Tess so much I could feel her skin on me.

I tried to tell myself that I only wanted her because someone else had her. I wasn't in love, just trapped in a competitive lust brought on by all the couple energy in the resort. I didn't want to do anything that remotely resembled settling down. I wanted to go on playing the field. I decided, right then, with raindrops running down my face, that if Celine asked, I would sleep with her again.

I nearly went back to dance, nearly went back to see if anyone wanted to take me to bed. But I knew if I did I'd close my eyes and pretend they were Tess.

Her throaty laughed flowed across the dark night, then her door was closed. The crackle of lightning got me moving up the stairs to my own door. I turned the bolt and stood in the dark for a long while, listening to the thunder but imagining I could still hear Tess's laugh.

Chapter Five

My alarm woke me from a dream so delicious I immediately wanted to go back to that wonderful place. It wasn't even a dream, it was a memory, and I closed my eyes. I drifted in between whacks on the snooze button, remembering the rest of that first night with Tess.

Tess had kept coming for me. I'd never been with a woman who could climax like that, and I had loved it.

"Yes," I crooned to her. "Let's get everything slippery and do that again, is that what you want?"

"Please," she hissed. "Please, Brandy. Fuck me again, please, I need it . . . please . . . "

I shushed her. "I'm not going to stop, sweetie."

"I'm sorry," she said again, and her eyes were again brimming with tears. "Sorry to be so—"

"I love it, I love that you want it and can ask me for it. Don't be sorry for liking this, or wanting it." With lube, I was able to slide into her again. She held me against her breasts for a few moments, then drew my lips to her tightening nipples.

I could feel her relax, feel her melt. It was fantastic. Every movement I made with my hips drew a sigh or a gasp. Our bodies were slick against each other and every time she lifted her pelvis to meet my thrust I felt dizzy with lust for her. Her nails raked over my back, my ribs, and I felt her spasm under me. It felt so good to know I was taking care of her itch, that I could be what she needed, and it was doubly pleasurable that every time she climaxed I got a little closer myself.

She was close again, and this time her cries were sharper, higher-pitched. I watched her face anxiously for any sign that I should slow but she never stopped groaning out "yes" as we moved. Then her legs were around my hips, crushing me until she shook under me so fiercely I could only hold on.

She was gasping so hard for breath I moved off of her. If she wanted more I'd be happy to oblige, but we both needed to cool off a little and drink some water. Her skin was flushed and eyes glassy in the way the trainer in me knew meant she was deprived of both oxygen and water.

"I'm just getting some ice," I told her. Remembering that she had been hurt by a guy who left without so much as a good-bye, I added, "I'm not leaving you."

She had caught her breath, mostly, when I handed her the tinkling glass. After several thirsty swallows, she sat up all the way. "I've never . . . never gone this far."

"How are you feeling?"

She gave me a sidelong glance. "Would you . . . could we . . . ?"

"Absolutely," I said. "I'm not going anywhere. Whatever you want."

She looked at me like she finally believed I wasn't going to leave her still wanting. "Whatever?"

"I'd be a fool not to agree to whatever you wanted." I'd finished half my glass of water and the curve of her hips was appealing to my mouth.

"Since you put it that way, I'd like you on your back this time."

"Oh." I was startled, but not unpleasantly. "You'll have no arguments from me."

She straddled my hips, just below the prominence of the toy. I thought she was reaching for the lube, but instead she got the glass, swishing water around in her mouth for several seconds. Then she was leaning over me and all in a rush took my breast into her cold mouth.

"Oh, damn . . . Tess . . . that feels fantastic."

The look she gave me could have started a forest fire. Her fingers dipped into her glass and several chilly drops sprinkled across my stomach. I arched involuntarily under her. "You seem to like that."

"It reminds me how alive I feel," I said.

"I've never felt more alive." She set the glass down and picked up the lube. I watched her moisten her hand, then wet the dildo with more of the wonderful slippery stuff. "Like what you see?"

Breathless, I watched her rise up until she could slip the toy inside her. With a visible shudder she settled down on it fully, closing her eyes. "Yes, I like what I see," I managed. I closed my eyes as the sensuous movement of her hips above mine made me arch in response.

Cold drops made my eyes open again. Tess had an ice cube in each hand. "Let's feel alive."

I was panting as I watched her delicately circle her nipples with the ice. They grew so red and swollen that I ached to bring them to my mouth. Then Tess was using the ice on mine and I moaned, overwhelmed with sensation. "God, you're sexy," I said. "You know what you want, what you like, and that turns me on."

She slipped what was left of one cube into my mouth and nothing had ever felt so refreshing. She likewise had the other cube in her mouth and then her cold fingers were trailing down my stomach. She leaned over me, her hips grinding on the toy.

"What?" I had to ask. I could hardly hear over the sound of my pounding heart.

"Fuck me, Brandy, fuck me until you come."

I really wanted to, but I wasn't sure how I was going to climax. She felt unbelievably good on top of me, and I had always loved this position, but I didn't know how I'd come, too. I worried, for a moment, that she was wishing I was a guy who could more easily have some sort of mutual orgasm, then all that went away. She sat up and arched her back, putting one hand behind her.

When I felt her fingertips opening my labia I shook with a contraction, and I fucked her, pushing up into her while her still cold fingers seemed to melt on my burning clit. I fucked her with hoarse little cries of my own need, holding her thighs. I gasped her name, over and over, while her touch on my clit drove me crazy. Then her sexy half-cry of climax—a sound I was fast learning to adore—washed over me and my own urgency welled up. We froze together for a moment, holding our breath, then Tess gave one last cry and crumpled on top of me.

She was crying and I didn't know if that was good or bad. I hoped it was good. I felt beyond great. Beyond wow, more than incredible.

"Was it okay?" She finally found some coherent words. Between sobs she searched my face for my answer.

"It was fabulous, *fabulous*, Tess. You were incredible. I've never felt so good with anyone before. It was okay that you wanted—"

"No, no. Was that last, was that okay? Was that good for you? I wanted you to get something out of it—"

"More than something, Tess, it was fantastic. Don't torture yourself. It was all wonderful." I cradled her head on my shoulder, feeling like a god of love. "Thank you for caring that I did . . . it would have been wonderful without, don't get me wrong. But I've never had anyone do that before."

She had laughed, the low easy laugh of the Tess I'd known for the last year. The tears had disappeared. "Like I said, you need a chick with long arms."

I rolled over in bed, replaying that moment when I'd felt her gather me inside her, not just the toy, but my needs, too. The times we'd been together since had been equally energetic. Unbelievably so. It had taken a few times before we'd remembered that sex could be had places other than the bed. Something inside me blossomed when I was with her. I felt grand, awesome, sexy, attractive—I felt better about me and who I was when she was there.

What had changed? I hit the snooze button one more time and asked myself why I felt so different today. We had been going along quite well, and the arrival of other lesbians on the scene had upset the balance, I guess. I kicked myself for not realizing Tess's interest in guys had always been somewhat weak. Sure, she talked pretty freely about sex, and had a long list of things she really liked, all of which were possible with the male of the species. But she never talked about a future where she got married, had kids and all that. Men touched her physically but now that I was considering the possibility that Tess might prefer women, I could see that either she didn't let men touch her more deeply, or they just didn't have what it took to reach inside her. Women did, maybe.

Maybe I did. Maybe I'd shown her that a door she'd never

considered was the very one she'd been looking for. But something was just not fair if in the end I fell in love with a straight woman who wasn't, only to lose her before she had even come out, lose her to a dyke she'd just met. None of that made much sense and it wasn't any fun at all to be living it.

Annoyed, I kicked off the covers and started my day. Shower, breakfast, Morning Stretch. I did not go to Tess's Body Pump because I had a two-hour stint at KidZone, one doing relief and the other working with five- to seven-year-olds on basic tumbling. On a day like today, my heart and head in turmoil, it was wonderful to lose myself in something so engrossing. Kids can be maddening, but they can also be refreshingly uncomplicated. Something hurts, they say so. Something pisses them off, you know about it right away. Something makes their heart fill with joy and you can see them grow right before your eyes.

I'd always thought I was in touch with my inner child. Like Celine had said, I wasn't in a hurry to grow up. So why couldn't I walk up to Tess and say, "I like hanging out with you. You make me feel great inside. I want you to be my best friend and to spend all my time with you. And I like that grown-up thing we do, too. I want to line up on the starting line and see if we're running a sprint or a marathon together. So how about it? Want to go steady and see if it's fun?"

Right.

I raced from the big tent to the main guest pool, arriving in time to do my bit in the dunk tank competition. I'd lost the draw this month. Stripped down to the sport bra and undies that passed successfully as a swimsuit, I perched on the wobbly apparatus that had been set up over the six-foot end of the main pool. Maybe it wouldn't be so bad, I thought. Usually the place was full of guys who just couldn't wait to show off their machismo. They'd let me barely get settled on the perch before throwing another pitch. The guests loved it, the kids loved it.

No guys this week, I told myself, and I relaxed on the perch.

Maybe it was the sun that made me forget about softball.

The first woman up slow-pitched me into the water five out of five balls. At least she let me get settled again, nice and safe, before launching the next salvo. It was a long line and I had to acknowledge that for all my genuine belief that lesbians were cooler in so many ways, they suffered from bouts of machismo, too. Ten times, then fifteen, and the line just kept getting longer.

A voice rang out from behind me. "Pick on someone your own size!" The entire apparatus swayed as someone else clambered on and I turned to see Alicia, costumed as Wonder Woman, brandishing her golden bracelets. The next ball missed and the one after hit the target square on, but I didn't drop.

"Wonder Woman to the rescue!" I shouted. Nobody but Alicia and me knew she'd set the safety latch to keep me out of the water. For a while everyone sort of bought the power of Wonder Woman saving my butt, but as looks grew suspicious Alicia kicked the latch off with an apologetic glance.

I took my time climbing back up from each tumble, but dykes are patient, especially softball dykes. It turned out there was a party of twelve from a softball league and damned if they weren't going to prove something.

The torture finally ended—lots of laughter and revelry, ha ha—and lunch couldn't have seemed more welcome. I pulled on my shorts and tank, not caring that I'd soak them through, and headed toward the dining room. I needed water most of all.

"That's the one," I heard a woman say as I went past. "The one who let Celine do her the first night."

"She is kinda cute . . . "

I kept walking, more because I was stunned than I was consciously choosing my actions. I could feel my face and shoulders burning a deep, angry red.

Had Celine told the world? Was everyone talking about us? Judging us?

Okay, I'd forgotten about softball dykes, and I'd forgotten about how dykes loved to classify, label and set up pyramids of righteousness, too. So I was the slut this week, apparently. Fine. Damn Celine for anything she'd said. Damn it, damn it. I'd been called a slut by men and I just didn't care. But I did care when it was dykes. Damned if I'd sleep with any of them now. Like they knew me, knew my life and had any business applying their definition of *slut* to me.

Blinking back tears I grabbed a banana and headed for my quarters. I had about an hour to myself, then there was a staff meeting before my two p.m. Body Pump class. Maybe I'd feel like eating something by then.

A tour group on JetSkis rounded the marina, heading for a landing at the sailing hut. The roar of their engines drowned out someone calling my name. Fuck and fuck it, it was Celine.

"Hey, wait up."

Fuming, I peeled the banana and starting eating it while I waited.

"I was wondering if you had plans for dinner." I took my time chewing and her cheerful expression faded. "Have I done something wrong?"

I shrugged. "Apparently I'm the one you did on the very first night."

She blinked, puzzled, then frowned. "Oh. Dyke gossip travels fast. Are you sorry we went to bed?"

"No," I muttered. "I just didn't expect to get a scarlet letter." I heaved a long sigh. "It was just a chance remark, but it bothered me."

"I haven't been out bragging," Celine assured me. "I don't do that. But people saw us leave together and I don't have an angel's reputation. Have dinner with me and stay to dance with me tonight and we'll really give them something to talk about."

I was tempted only because she offered something easy and uncomplicated by anything but lust. I didn't feel lustful, though. At least not toward Celine. But if I refused, would Celine think I was, in fact, a one-night stand only? We'd hardly talked, and damn, I had admired the woman for years. I'd forgotten she was Celine Griffin, in fact.

I went for honesty. "Well, yes to dinner, I'd like that. I don't know about dancing, though. This is my longest workday of the week."

"Don't you get days off?"

"Half-days Wednesday afternoons and Friday mornings."

"Wow. Okay, I understand. We'll see about dancing, then." She stepped closer and I could smell her appealing cologne. Saturday night *had* been really wonderful. "If you've strength for things other than dancing, I can forgo the disco, believe me." I guess some of my surprise must have shown, because she quickly added, "Did you really think I wouldn't want to see you again if I could?"

I shrugged. "Last night, I didn't get that idea. I wasn't hurt or anything—"

"I thought you'd come back from the bar and we'd polish the parquet."

"Oh." I smiled a little. "I didn't understand."

She affected outrage. "Did you really think I couldn't handle a pissy D.J. on my own? I was trying to figure how to lure you there."

I laughed outright. "Okay, I missed it. I was preoccupied, maybe."

"With me, I hope." Her hands were on my hips and all the chemistry that had worked between us before became very pronounced. I was single, wasn't I? Couldn't I follow the wise advice of pagans: an' it hurts no one, do as ye will?

I don't know what I would have done one way or the other, but Tess walked past us then. Her glance at me held no amusement. It was almost disdain. It wasn't like Tess at all.

Stung, I called, "Hey, Tess?" She turned for a moment. "If you take my Body Pump this afternoon, I'll take yours in the morning."

Her gaze slid from me to Celine to Celine's hands on my hips, then rose slightly to my obviously hard nipples. I could have told her it was my wet sport bra causing that, but it was no longer entirely true. "Sure," she said, not meeting my gaze again. "I've got a hot date and this way we can sleep in."

Tess hurried off and Celine pulled me closer. "Do I understand that you are free until three now? That's about ninety minutes."

I nodded and we stared at each other. Tess had a date, I told myself. I flashed on the vision of her unbuttoned blouse.

Celine whispered in my ear, "How would you feel about a naughty, needy, raunchy afternoon fuck?"

We hit the wall just inside my door and I didn't even have time to be glad I'd cleaned up a little. Celine was pulling off my shirt and bra and I had my hand down her shorts while she did it. My response to her was complicated, I knew that. Not just physical—she was hot and wet and wanted me—but also because I trusted her to be Celine. I trusted her to fuck me and let me fuck her, and to leave on Saturday so that I could go on with my life. As much as I wanted Tess at that moment, Tess wasn't safe for my heart or my sanity. I knew the rules with Celine.

One of the rules was to like it, and I did like it. I liked it a lot. Her teeth were raising my nipples to even harder points and I was cupping her ass as we writhed against the wall. Sometimes her back was to it, and sometimes mine was. In one of those times when she was the one with spread thighs, panting against me and thrusting against my hand, her legs threatened to give out.

"Can we get to the bed?" She had one hand on her forehead, as if she was dizzy.

"Sure," I murmured.

She pulled me down on top of her and I remembered how she liked it. I was inside her, no teasing, no holding back. Hard and fast, four fingers deep. She arched up with a sustained groan and I was lost in the dance of her smooth, dark thighs across my crumpled white sheets.

So female. I love women.

So beautiful. I love curves and soft and muscles and cunts, wet, hot cunts that ripple in response to being touched.

It felt good inside her and when we finally came to a rest, her arms around my waist while we laughed breathlessly, I felt like maybe I had gotten beyond the "must have Tess to feel good" frame of mind. What did I care if Tess was with some woman this week? On Saturday Bleachie and Celine would leave and Tess and I would be back to where we'd been.

Celine, looking sexier by the minute, flipped me, but it wasn't like I resisted. Her fingers began a delicious exploration of my body and I spread myself out, luxuriating in the feel of her touch. I was with Celine Griffin, famous lesbian and, in my book, sex goddess.

"Oh, that does feel fine, doesn't it?" She was moving on top of me, nudging my legs farther and farther apart. I wanted her fingers as far inside me as they would go.

The phone rang.

Celine froze and I found myself holding my breath. Two long rings, then a third, all indicating it was a call from outside the resort. My antiquated answering machine whirred into action.

"I never get calls," I said. Her fingers were right at my opening, but the passion of the moment was teetering.

It was completely lost when I heard my mother's voice.

I sat bolt upright, nearly knocking Celine to the floor. "Holy shit!"

Distorted by the speaker, my mother's voice was reedy and weak. "I know we haven't spoken in so long, dear—"

I retorted to the machine, "Yeah, how about because you told me I was a pervert!"

"—in times of emergency, family has to forgive and come together. Your father would have wanted you here. It's hard to believe he's gone. It was very sudden . . . he'd given up smoking and started exercising . . . but . . . too little . . . "

Reeling, I clambered out of bed and stumbled toward the phone. "I'm here," I said. What else was there to say?

"Oh, I'm glad, Brandy. I wasn't sure this number would still reach you. It was a stroke, dear. The funeral is Wednesday afternoon. Will you come home?"

"When did it happen?" She sounded so frail, but it wasn't the first time that weak little Mom had used it for guilt. Maybe she'd changed. I'd heard that people did sometimes change.

"Saturday. I've just . . . been in shock. Your brother is managing the details. I don't know what I'd do without him."

That was Roger, dutiful and appreciated. A ticket would cost a fortune but what else was there to say but, "I'll be there. I don't know when, but I will be there."

My mother's voice firmed up a lot and she said, more like the mother I remembered, "I'm glad, dear. You do have something black? If you need a hat for church, don't worry, I have plenty. Come by the house first and we'll go to the church in Uncle Bert's Town Car."

I counted to five, then said, "I'll be there. I have to go make arrangements."

"Very well." Now very much the mother I remembered, she hung up without the wasted time of a good-bye.

Celine had quietly come up behind me, and her arms were strong and comforting. "I'm so sorry," she said softly.

"He was a bastard," I answered flatly. "I let him down the day I was born without a penis, and things only got worse when he decided he'd teach me, over and over, that I wasn't a boy. They had a boy the second time, though. Lucky, huh?"

"Do you have to go?"

Not going hadn't occurred to me. "Yes. I mean, even though Mom called and asked me to go, she really doesn't want me there. If it weren't for the circumstances the uptight, freaked-out church ladies would rather I wasn't there either. Maybe that's why I have to go."

Celine nodded as if that made sense, though I wasn't sure it did. "Do you want me to leave? You must have things to do now."

"No—it's okay. I mean, I don't feel like . . . "

She turned me to face her. "Of course not." She gave me an intent look. "I gather you were estranged."

"Yeah. I came out to them and it was good-bye to me forever. I haven't spoken to them for two years."

"That must have been rough."

I shrugged. "Like everybody else, I got a job and figured out how to take care of myself."

"Are you okay?"

I shrugged again. "I'm angry, I guess." I was, too, so angry I felt numb. I'd talked to Tess about my parents and brother and suddenly I wanted her, propped up on the sofa, a brownie in one hand while the other played in her hair as she talked. She knew all the gory details. She wouldn't have to ask questions. She knew . . . me.

"I guess I do need to go. I need to ask for leave and use a computer in the office to book a ticket. Shower first, I guess."

Celine nodded. "A good plan. Let me just find all my clothes. I know one sock is under the bed. Your room is just like mine. I hadn't realized."

"Yeah, instead of a second bed we have that kitchenette kind of thing."

"You can pop your own popcorn while you watch a movie at least."

My laugh was unamused. "Yeah, with all the free time."

"Oh, right. I forgot. Your hours are ridiculous."

I felt as if our conversation was being conducted at the end of a long hallway. "It's a living."

She was mostly dressed by the time I had gathered a small pile of items I was worriedly thinking I would need to pack. I was pulling my only suitcase, which doubled as an overflow laundry basket, out of the rear of the closet while she tied her shoelaces. "Listen, Brandy, I realize you might have to leave abruptly, so if I don't see you . . . I'm sorry we didn't get to finish what we started."

I tried for a smile. "At some point I think I'm going to be sorry too."

"Maybe someday we'll get to finish things up. I like being with you. It's been . . . "

"Uncomplicated?" She nodded slowly, and I added, "We both like what we like."

"And we didn't have to negotiate the harness and discuss if I was being het-centric. Or if my getting off by holding you down was deep-seated violent tendencies toward women."

I found myself grinning, though it felt like someone else's body. "I bet that gets old."

"Ruins the mood, too. Look . . . in case I don't see you

again." She pulled me close and kissed me gently, almost maternally, on the forehead. "Here's some advice from an old broad. Dance through life any way you want, and don't worry about people who can't hear the music."

"Thank you." I didn't tell her I recognized the sentiment from her stand-up special three or four years ago. I appreciated that the advice had been well-intentioned. "I'm still not sure I want to grow up."

"Oh, you have, you're just queen of the party barge."

I closed the door after she left, shaking my head. I was not living in the land of denial. I was free of the crushing weight of material possessions like china sets and Town Cars. I didn't have to spend Sundays, afternoons and evenings all week discussing God and Country. I spent most of my day doing work that I enjoyed. I had no mortgage to meet and no concerns about where my next meal was coming from. Two years ago it had seemed like a perfect choice.

Reality was intruding. I was starting to think maybe I had a heart that could be caught by one woman and that thought had never crossed my mind before. I also had a credit card that would be just about maxed out with the price of an air ticket. A savings account with more than a few dollars would have been a big help.

Was this how growing up began? Life asked a little more from you than you could easily manage so you changed? Had I been on a surfboard all this time, working my way out from shore, and now I had to turn around and ride the waves—all the highs, and all the lows—back in?

What would be waiting for me on the shore when I got in? What did I want there? If life was a marathon, how would I recognize the milestones?

I dashed away an angry tear as I made the bed, then got in the shower. Damn my father and his pissant fire-and-brimstone preachings. He'd said I slept with other girls to make God angry, to get God's attention, and since in our house he was God, well, that meant I was sleeping with other girls to get his attention. That was my father in a nutshell. Even my sleeping with girls was somehow about him.

I wanted Tess. I really needed her. She'd know what to say. She'd tell me I was okay to feel mad and hurt that I never got to tell the old bastard to go to hell before he actually went there. I got soapsuds in my mouth laughing at the thought of him arriving in his worst nightmare hell, filled with gruesome specters of all that he hated: feminists, drag queens and dark-skinned people who didn't "talk American." I hoped that's where he was. As far as I was concerned, it was where he deserved to be.

Randall was actually decent to me. First time ever he didn't do or say something to make me either mad or resentful. "The policy is three days' paid leave for bereavement, but if you need a few more than that to help your mother, then I could easily cover you for five or six days. I'm really sorry about your loss, Brandy."

I knew he could tell I'd been crying, and damn it, I had to keep swallowing to be able to speak. I was so angry I couldn't see. "Thank you. I appreciate knowing that."

"You go book a flight and I'll let people know you'll be taking off."

He followed me as I left his office and said something to Rosa, the reception manager. Rosa enveloped me in a gardenia hug and said she had booked flights on the Internet before and would happily give me a hand.

I screwed with it for an hour, trying to find a flight combination that would fit on my credit card. I was cursing my father under my breath as I narrowed the search down to an itinerary that went from Tampa to Dallas, where I waited for nearly four hours, then on to Baltimore. That journey cost two hundred dollars less than Tampa to Atlanta to Baltimore. Even so, my credit card couldn't handle the nearly eight-hundred-dollar charge.

I glanced at the clock. I supposed there was enough time to get to my bank, withdraw my meager savings and pay down my credit card balance enough, but I was willing to bet that wouldn't take effect until tomorrow, when the ticket would probably cost even more.

Damn it, I thought. If my mother had called me yesterday I could have rented a car and been halfway there, comfortably. The only way I'd get there in time now would be a long haul, and I'd have to arrange for a car and leave tonight. It would be much cheaper, and I wouldn't have to commit to a return date. Those extra days off Randall had just offered me meant I wouldn't have to hurry to get back. A car would be far more convenient. Besides, I was willing to bet no one would pick me up at the airport so I'd have to pay for shuttles and have no control over where I went and when.

My mind made up, I clicked back to the start page and selected car rentals. Anything that got decent mileage and had a CD player would do.

A throat was cleared behind me and I turned to see Rosa smiling shyly. She held out a bulging white envelope. "You always help out when anyone needs a little bit. Believe me, not everyone does. So now we can finally pay you back, though we all wish it weren't under these circumstances. You'll need it, or your mama will."

Stunned, I took the envelope. I hadn't expected it. Sure, when the hat was passed for backroom staff I chipped in. I might not make much money, but I lived for nearly free. Sure, I didn't get the tips they made, but I also didn't get furloughed for a week if the number of guests was low. "Rosa, I don't know what to say."

"You don't need to say a thing—"

"Thank you. Thank everybody, please? I'm going to drive, I think. I can get there in time and it's so much less expensive."

"Marguerite in the kitchen said if you call you could get maybe half off on a flight for bereavement. You need to know the name of the funeral home so they can verify."

I thought about it for a moment. Half was still four hundred dollars and once I was there I'd be marooned unless I rented a car anyway. "I still think I'll drive. I like driving."

"Then you use the money to stay someplace nice on the way, where they'll bring you breakfast in bed the way you did Lise when she broke her ankle."

Blinking really fast and hard didn't stop the tears. "This makes a huge difference. Thank you." I wouldn't have to use my credit card for eleven hundred miles' worth of gas. Wiping my face, I gestured at the screen. "So I'm looking at car rentals."

"No, no," she said. She reached for the phone. "*Mi hermano* works for Hertz."

Walking back to my quarters felt strange. I was out of my usual rhythm. My body knew it was after four on a Monday, and it was time for tumbling lessons with the eight to ten kids. I also knew that right now Tess was doing weight room instruction for guests wanting to plan routines on the fitness equipment. I realized that if I hadn't asked her to take my Body Pump class I might have missed my mother's call.

I took the time to tuck the cash-filled envelope into my suitcase. I was still stunned by everyone's generosity. I hated my father and he was dead and I had three hundred dollars out of the blue. It would easily get me there and back, and maybe I could stay someplace nice and watch a movie in the room, almost like a vacation.

It would take some thinking to work through the irony of it all.

Feeling more than a little bemused, I decided work would clear my head. My heart wanted to veer left to the fitness center, though, where I could at least look at Tess, then tell her the news, if she hadn't heard. But my feet kept plodding onward until I was under the circus tent.

Rajid tried to shoo me away. "You're covered. Go take care of you."

"This is taking care of me," I said. "Rosa's got a rental car being delivered. Randall gave me time off. I need distraction or I'll just spend the next few hours remembering all the reasons my father and I weren't speaking."

With a glance at the kids, Rajid said simply, "Family is as family does. No more, no less."

There was only a half-hour left, but working with smaller groups of kids was always more effective. Rajid handled cartwheels and I took over dive-and-rolls. At five we marched the kids back to KidZone where I got lovely hugs from Rhea and the other staffers. I usually had dinner now, with Tess, so I went that direction at my usual pace.

I wanted to run, though, do anything to find her seconds sooner so she could hold me and I could cry. Dignity made me put my hands in my pockets and stroll. I had no cares, no worries. I was calm.

Until I saw her, that is. Until I looked up and saw her hurrying toward me, her eyes sad and her arms open.

Any other week we might not have stood there for several minutes, just holding each other close, but it wasn't as if these guests would find it odd. It was a surprising feeling, standing in the open air, in plain sight of the world, and holding Tess as close as physically possible.

"I'm sorry, sweetie," Tess murmured in my ear, over and over. "So sorry."

Her body was warm, and the smell of her—soap, deodorant, shampoo, spray, whatever made it up—was welcome. I breathed her in, holding her very tight. I didn't want to let go.

"Have you eaten anything?"

"Not really."

"Let's get some sandwiches and eat at your place. You can pack and we can talk."

I nodded and realized I had to consciously make my arms let go of her.

"There you are, Brandy!" Rosa was bearing down on us. "The car is here, but you need to sign the contract."

"I'll get the food and let myself into your place," Tess said quickly. "I'm glad that the LOVE people are performing tonight."

I followed Rosa back to reception. My father would likely have been thrilled to know the timing of his death robbed me of several days in lesbian company. I was going to miss Celine Griffin's performance on Friday night unless I busted my butt to get back. In fact, most of the LOVE women would be gone by the time I returned. Depressed in addition to being angry, I signed the paperwork and then headed for my quarters and Tess.

"I was going to swipe some wine." She'd set out the sandwiches and chilled bottles of water. "But if you're heading out tonight you shouldn't drink."

"It has to be tonight if I want more than a few hours of sleep along the way."

"You should take a nap before you leave. Eat a decent dinner and then have a nap." She set the wrapped sandwiches down on the tiny kitchen table. "If you want I'll wake you later."

She was probably right about the nap. I ate some of the ham and cheese hoagie because she pointed at it and said I should. Food did help. I didn't feel quite so blue.

"I was realizing that I'm going to miss the rest of the week of the women."

"That sucks, really. Another reason to hate your dad?"

"Yeah, he'd be pleased if he knew. I'm so angry, Tess. So angry that I can hardly feel it."

She chewed thoughtfully, then suggested, "Because he never cared a thing about you? Smacked you around sometimes?"

"No, that's old." I swallowed with difficulty. "I'm still mad about that, but right now it's all such a jumble. It's not fair that I never got a chance to make him see what a shit he was. He slammed the door in my face and I never had the ovaries to say, 'Fuck you too, you hypocrite.'"

I had another thought, a very unwelcome one. I managed a swallow of water while Tess patted my hand.

"I'll never get to prove him wrong about me. I'll never be able to show him I was a success at something when he said I'd do nothing but fail. I didn't realize . . . " My eyes filled with hot tears.

"Didn't realize you still wanted to prove him wrong? That his opinion still mattered?"

I nodded mutely.

Very softly, she said, "Your life wasn't the way it's supposed to be. Neither was mine. I think about what my life might have been like if my folks hadn't died. You know, like on *Star Trek*? I can see the parallel universe, and that makes me really sad. Well, it used to. Nothing I could have done would have fixed it and . . . I guess what I mean is, if your father had lived to be a hundred you couldn't have fixed it. Only he could fix him. You can only fix you. The hard part is not letting the anger and frustration turn you into him or your mom."

"You mean he's done me a favor? I can stop wasting energy on him now? How ironic, the last thing he ever did was something good for me." I scrubbed my face with a napkin.

Tess pushed the rest of her sandwich to one side. "Hard as it is to accept, nothing your father ever did was about you. A teacher I once had said there is nothing so profoundly insulting as to be seen as irrelevant."

"I was stupid to waste my time on him to begin with. He never cared what I did unless it was wrong. Then he made sure I knew about it."

She reached for my fingers, her thumb smoothing over the nearly invisible scar on the back of my hand. Tess knew about the brick he'd let fall on it to teach me a lesson about not being alert. It had taught me never to take my eyes off him. Even when I wasn't looking at him I was.

"I'm really sorry, Brandy. But yeah, maybe you can get some peace. Don't go for him or your mom. Go for you and then wipe your feet on the way out."

I cupped her hand in mine. Tess was the first person I'd told about my parents who hadn't suggested that I should try to reconcile with them. "I'm glad you're here."

Our gazes met. Her blue-gray eyes were shimmering with sympathetic tears. With a hard swallow, she released my hand and went back to her sandwich. "What are you going to wear?"

I pointed at the bed. "The only black dresses I have are too short, so it'll be black slacks and that black blouse and my leather jacket. I can't get around that. I'm not going to try terribly hard either."

She moved to the sofa while I finished packing. I was probably taking too much, but I didn't want to have to waste money on silly things I already had, like aspirin and shampoo. Once the suitcase was zipped I joined her on the sofa.

She took my hand as I settled down. Her fingers traced a delicate pattern along my forearm. "So, I guess all your relatives will be there."

"Yeah. I'm to go to the house first to make sure I'm properly attired. I need a hat for church."

"What, a Club Sandzibel ballcap won't cut it?"

"Nah, it has to be this little lacy thing that perches right on top. Small, but conspicuous in its piety. Only women with blue hair wear them."

"You'll be fine."

"They'll all stare." I shrugged. I felt so much better holding her hand and having her close. Suddenly exhausted, I closed my eyes. "They'll all stare and . . . "

"Bran?"

I started awake. "Sorry—"

"No, it's okay, just move a little bit . . . there." My head came to a rest against her shoulder. "I'll wake you."

"Okay." At least I think I said it aloud.

My next conscious thought was that it was dark and my cheek pressed against something soft. I stirred slightly and found my head was in Tess's lap. She was asleep, her head resting on the back of the sofa.

I looked, long and hard, and my head was crowded with a jumble of feelings. I needed to leave for home, but this was home. Home was where she was, but I had to leave her. I didn't want to go. I wanted to stay right where I was, surrounded by the reality of her.

I carefully sat up, not wanting to wake her—but hoping she would wake up on her own. The room was dark, but the open curtains let in light from the courtyard. Looking at her I felt the same wonderful, terrifying mix of emotions that I'd felt the day Susan Porkland had asked if she could touch my breasts. It felt just like that moment in time, when I'd realized that I wasn't the only girl who liked to touch other girls. Pure magic. Nothing since had seemed so innocent, but I felt that way right now, looking at Tess's face in the soft, low light.

I made a small noise, back in my throat. I didn't know what to call this feeling, no word seemed quite right.

Her eyes fluttered open and she slowly lifted her head. Completely dressed, I felt naked. I breathed out her name so softly I wasn't sure she heard me.

It was only a few seconds that we stared at each other, but the spaces in between the beats of my heart were overflowing with feeling.

She leaned forward and I realized what she was going to do. Something she had never done before.

She kissed me. Full on the lips. Sweet, soft, tender and something more. I was stunned. She kissed me like a lover would. We'd done a lot of things together, but never this, and this kiss seemed the most intimate touch of all.

When we had to stop to breathe she just looked at me and then I kissed her and our mouths opened and it was delicious and welcome and heated. When her hand came to the back of my neck I melted into her body and we kissed, over and over. I felt like I was making up for lost time, thinking this was how I should have kissed her that first night, and how I had wanted to kiss her the last time we were together, but kisses hadn't been something we shared. They were about love and we were about sex and hormones and friendly physical sharing. Weren't we?

This wasn't about hormones, or backrubs, or being buddies. She wanted me. I could feel it in her shivering skin and hear it in the rising level of the soft noise she made every time our mouths parted and then found each other again.

There was a low, gray murmur inside me, about things I needed to do, and cars and maps and anger. It was far away, someplace else. The rest of me was in Tess's arms, and when she brought her hands to my waist to pull me even closer all I could hear was the pounding of my heart and those little sounds she was making as she kissed me.

We kissed as I slowly sank onto my back, pulling her down with me.

"Are you sure?" We whispered the question to each other at the same moment, then stopped to smile our answers. Clothes slipped out of the way and we sighed together as our nipples brushed. Then I felt her pubic hair tangling with mine and we began to move together, rolling our hips in a slow, comfortable rhythm.

She was on top of me as my legs slowly parted. I wanted her, but not like all the times before with her. Not like she had my prescription and was kindly filling it. I wanted her like a lover. I wanted her to moan as loudly as I did when her fingers discovered how wet I was.

And when they did, when I felt her part my lips and slip into the heat there, she did moan. She moaned into my mouth as we kissed and I felt her skin heat up and I knew she wanted me. I thought, ridiculously, that I was being made love to for the first time in my life.

We had always talked before, said low, sweaty things about how good skin and sweat and friction and wet felt, but tonight we were without words in the dark. I didn't need any words. It was clear she knew what every small movement of my body meant.

She slid inside me so easily that the part of me that usually gasped or moaned didn't respond. Instead, I felt lit from within by different fires, and they were burning hotter and higher with every stroke of her fingers inside me. I was giving something up to her though I could not name what it was.

She moaned quietly as the inside of me began to flutter and then she was pushing deeper. Deeper, filling me, and I wanted her to touch places inside me, secret and private. Places that weren't physical, though her fingers were how she would reach them. Not just reach, but stroke, caress. She was making love to the inside of me.

"Is this okay?"

I started as if from sleep. I had only felt her hand, as if it were the only way we connected. But there were her eyes, anxious but loving, and her mouth, a passionate curve of desire.

"Yes, it's more than . . . please . . . "

She pushed deeper again and my eyes widened in response. The look on her face was one of awe and astonishment. "You've never felt like this—"

"You've never touched me like this, with your hand so deep—"

"I've wanted to—"

"Love me . . . Love me, Tess, the way you want to."

She leaned over my vibrating body, her hair cloaking us so that every word seemed to be captured in our private world. "I am making love to you, and now, now I'm going to fuck you."

"Please!"

"Do you feel that?"

She pulled her fingers out of me, then sank in again, and I felt stretched and full and enveloping her even as she covered me with her body. Then she kissed me, frantically, hungrily, kissed me while she fucked me, and told me yes.

Whatever the questions were, the answer was yes between us at that moment, and those secret, private places inside me opened to the light of her.

I was hot inside, hot from her touch, her light, hot but not burning. Burning would hurt and nothing she had ever done had hurt me. Hot, like muscles thrilling to a climb, like my heart driving me to run faster, lift more, just because I could. Hot, inside my cunt, inside my breasts, inside my head. When the explosions began, coming for her was the most natural thing I had ever done.

Tess was still inside me, and I felt her tears on my stomach. Everything changed. She was the soothing cool to bring me down, the limitless wet of a woman.

I kissed her panting mouth and pushed her hair out of her eyes. Our faces and lips were damp. My tongue was thirsty for her tears, for the inside of her mouth. I knew what I wanted.

I let my tongue suggest it. I trailed it along her neck, then flicked lightly over her breasts. I coiled my tongue around her erect nipple, and she gasped. We were slowly shifting positions so she was on her back and I was stretched out between her legs. I could smell her and I wanted to fill my mouth with the most beautiful part of her.

"I don't want to ask this," I whispered. "I don't want you to think I'm just being bitchy and jealous. But did . . . you . . . she . . . ?"

Tess blinked, her expression puzzled.

"How safe do I need to be? I want to go down . . . " I paused, feeling shy. I could tell Tess I was going to hold her down and fuck her greedy cunt, but it was suddenly very difficult to say simply that I wanted to taste her cunt with my tongue, and do that for, oh, several hours.

"We didn't do that. Just her fingers," Tess whispered back. "She . . . Oh, hell, Brandy. What the heck is stone?"

I laughed and it broke the immediate mood. She smiled weakly and there she was, the Tess I loved, my best friend, the woman I could say just about anything to. "She didn't want you to touch her back?"

Tess shook her head. "I thought there was something wrong with me the first time, and the second, well, I thought she was really turned on, but . . . "

"It wasn't you. Some women choose that. They like to touch, but not be touched back."

"Oh." She blinked. "There was a guy I dated for a while in

116

college who liked to do me until I came, but he didn't except every . . . like fifth time. He said once he'd gone two years."

"I think that's Tantric sex. For him at least."

"Oh."

"Tess?" She looked at me and I moved against her pelvis. "The important thing right now is that I'm not stone, and neither are you. And I want to bury my face between your legs and stay there."

She drew a sharp breath. "You've never—"

"I've wanted to, so much. But I thought you were with guys and—oh, yes, yes, I will."

"No more talking," she said in that voice of hers that made me want to devote every breath to her pleasure. Her hand was twined in my hair and she was pushing me down. I let her guide my face to her and pull me in. I loved the feel of her hand on the back of my head. I was submerged in the fathomless ocean of her and she held me there without moving.

She tasted so good, and she was copiously wet. Dyke ego asserted itself. I coiled my tongue around her clit and her hand dropped away from my head. Her legs went limp. She got impossibly more wet and let out a long coo that I'd never heard from her before.

Running my tongue just along the sides, I felt her clit elongate and stiffen in response. Tess was groaning and I settled comfortably on my stomach, arms around her legs, as I gloried in her intricate ripples.

I tasted all of her, inside and out, side to side, coating my lips, nose, cheeks. I loved kissing her labia and whipping my tongue through every furled fold of her. Whenever she lifted her knees I felt as if she was offering herself, for me to go inside. My tongue was no match for the size of the toys she preferred, but her legs jerked in response as I teased her opening, then slipped past it to tease. When her knees relaxed again I would swoop up to her clit, catching it between my lips to pinch it, just a little. Her knees would lift and it would all begin again until her hoarse gasps took on that familiar edge of nearly there. Nearly ... almost ...

I was thinking that when she was hormonal she liked to be held down, but she'd said the rest of the time she was a "slow, easy screw." I wanted her to come but didn't know her body this way. She could get hyperstimulated or anxious—and now I was anxious. I wanted her to come, to feel the wonderful splendid cascade of feeling that being loved this way could bring. At least it always had for me.

Her voice changed and I knew that small nuance. She was nearly there, almost, and starting to worry she wouldn't get the rest of the way.

Dyke ego said no guy had ever done this right, and dyke ego said she did like what I was doing, but maybe she couldn't come this way and we were both going to get frustrated by my continuing to try. She'd think I was disappointed if she didn't and maybe I would be, a little, but more than anything, I wanted that hoarse cry of hers to break out of her throat, the way it did when she was in the throes. I didn't care how she got there. I had loved her the best I could, and now what really mattered was that she get release and the assurance that I had loved touching and licking her. And I had, every moment of it.

I freed my hands from their tight grasp of her legs and reached up for her forearms. She groaned as I tightened my grip, pulling her firmly down against my face.

"I love this part of you." I felt tears stinging my eyes. "I love your wet pussy in my mouth."

She groaned again, loudly, and I let go of her arms to seize her legs. Scrambling to my knees I pushed her legs up until her thighs were on her stomach. She was completely exposed. I trailed my nipples across the taut, swollen flesh, and then went back with my mouth, sucking her clit between my lips. I slipped one finger just inside her opening, rubbing lightly there where she'd responded to my tongue. I was about to go deeper when she wrapped her arms around her knees and cried out. Everything got wet as she rocked and writhed and I did exactly what I was doing, exactly that, until she finally began to relax.

I let her legs fall and clambered up to kiss her and hold her tight against me. "That was amazing. You tasted so good. I loved doing that, and then the way you came, that was—"

She kissed me, either out of gratitude or to shut me up, I didn't care.

After a while, when the kisses slowed, words spilled over us. Our voices were tangled and low and if we made sense I couldn't fathom it. It was sweet and quiet, and I was aware all at once of the profound beauty of our mutual tenderness.

Chapter Six

I was pleased she went back to sleep. It was easier to leave. I didn't want to go. I wanted her to come with me, that was what I wanted. Life made more sense when I was with her. But that wasn't going to happen at midnight and the journey was not getting any shorter. I covered her with the comforter from my bed, wrote a note that part of me hoped she wouldn't find, and quietly took a shower.

The village was settling down and quiet as I slipped out the door. I said good-bye to the guard at the gate and popped a CD into the player of the little fuel-efficient Geo. Even as the bounce of a club mix washed over me, all my thoughts were with the woman I'd left sleeping on my sofa. I wanted to wake her and love her again, enjoy the soft, sleepy need of her body, the sweet warmth of her smile, and the insights of her laughing mind.

We had made love, and it was different than everything we'd done before. It was different than anything I'd felt with anyone else. I'd had good, bad and mediocre sex, but even the very best, like with Celine, hadn't felt like that. I wanted to do it again, and again.

I was torn about her finding the note. There was no taking it back. I had first written just my mother's home phone number and the word *Emergency*.

Then I'd wished for a Hallmark card or something that would be far more eloquent that I would ever manage. Something had changed between us and I was scared to put it into words.

I am coming back, I'd written. *I want breakfasts and silly hearts and valentines. We can talk about it when I get back.*

The Geo's tires thumped in rhythm as I drove across the causeway that separates Sanibel Island from Fort Meyers. Before I was really aware of any distance at all, I was merging onto I-75 and settling in for the first leg of the trip.

I'd driven it before, just once, right after I got the job at Club Sandzibel. I don't know what I'd expected, but my parents' chilly reception, and my brother's open contempt for my job, had ended any desire on my part to go back. When I had the chance to sell my fume-belching Firebird, which needed a new ring something or other, I'd taken the deal.

In the dark all of Florida looks the same. That might sound silly, but the interstates run through nowhere. Once I'd skirted Tampa and turned northeast on I-4, there was nothing to look at but the lights on other cars all the way to Kissimmee.

I changed CDs several times, and at the outskirts of Orlando thought irrelevantly that someday I'd like to go to Disney World. I was willing to bet that I was going to get asked if I'd been, given that I lived in Florida. I don't think most people realized how big the state is, and that toll roads and two-lane highways with low speed limits made getting around tedious. Rajid, who had lived in Los Angeles for several years, said that Californians thought nothing of a hundred-mile daily commute, and the only tolls they paid were to cross bridges. In Florida, a hundred-mile drive required days of planning, maps, a cup full of quarters and a supply of bottled water.

I realized I didn't have any water and was instantly thirsty.

I took my first break at a bustling truck stop near Daytona Beach where campers, truckers and tourists alike mingled. It felt safe and I bought several bottles of water and a few packets of nuts. I ought to have raided the dining room for fruit, but I hadn't been thinking earlier. Gas was more expensive than I thought, and I was more grateful than ever for the envelope of crumpled folding money. My coworkers, many of whom I couldn't say more than hello to in their own language, had shown me more consideration than my family had.

I'd read in plenty of places about how gay people create their own families, and build communities to compensate for their families of origin, blah blah blah. Well, the laugh was on me, because for the first time I had an inkling what that all meant. *Community* had always seemed abstract to me. Now I got it. When life shoved you off balance, your community was the steadying hand. When something happened that flattened you, your family was the people who'd pick you up, ply you with chicken soup, alcohol or chocolate and set you back on your feet.

Maybe I could figure out *family* and *community*, but . . . *relationship*? I was in love with Tess, but the idea of a relationship was completely foreign. Nobody stayed together these days, and those that did were like my parents. Look what marriage had done for them. My father had slept with his secretaries and my mother knew the words "yes, dear" and that was about it.

Why try? If there was no happily forever, why even make a

commitment? I didn't really understand why anybody—including gay people—wanted to get married. Wasn't a wedding vow these days just, "I'll stay until I don't feel like it anymore"?

And yet I wanted to make promises to Tess. I wanted to be bound in some way because what I was feeling inside was so huge, and so magnificent, and so scary, that pretending it wasn't there would destroy it, as well as parts of me that might not let that feeling ever grow again.

In the rest stop bathroom I glanced at myself in the mirror, surprised.

I didn't look any different. Same eyes, same wild hair. Same nose, same ears. I didn't look like a woman in love. For the first time in years, though, I thought the outside of me didn't quite fit the inside. My hair still looked like high school. I wanted something else, something that said that I was in love, and with a woman, and that it was the most marvelous feeling in the world. I totally understood why straight men liked women—women are just the *best*. I wanted to look in the mirror and see that truth emblazoned on me somehow.

Thing is, I didn't know what that would look like. I just knew when I put on the black clothes and the stupid hat for church, I was going to look even less like I felt on the inside.

The sun was teasing the horizon when I crossed into Georgia on I-95, and I had a greasy, overdue breakfast in Hardeeville, South Carolina. The place was busy but the grits were good. There was a little market adjoining the diner and I stocked up on bananas, oranges and Slim Jims. No long car journey was complete without an extruded, extra salty mystery meat product.

I knew Tess was up. I wondered if she was doing Morning Stretch, or if Moika was doing it because Tess would have two Body Pumps to lead. I wondered if Tess had found my note. What had I meant? What was I asking for? For her not to be with anyone while I was gone, even though she was walking around a buffet of female treasures? Did I care about other women, given that last night we had shared something incredible that I doubted I'd feel with anyone else?

I guess I did care. I don't know. Her body was her own. I wanted more than just her body. The highway was boring and I pictured Tess with Celine, getting fucked the way I had been. Would Tess give up an encounter like that for me?

The bigger question was, I suppose, would I give up the Celine Griffins for Tess? Yes. No.

Yes. No. *Relationship*. I just didn't get it.

By the time I got to North Carolina I had Tess in bed with woman after woman, learning what stone butch and pillow queen and flippable top meant. She'd learn all the labels and wonderful secrets about how women made love. When I got back I would be just another dyke in her life. She'd forget all about me, forget all about the way we'd been last night.

She wouldn't want me.

For the next two hundred miles that was all I heard, going around in my head like the sound of the tires on the asphalt. *She wouldn't want me*. The only variety was the equally unwelcome *And why would she?*

I pulled off the road at noon in Dunn, North Carolina, bought a Snickers from the rest stop vending machine, then waited a few minutes for a parking space in the scant shade. Windows rolled up and doors locked, I made myself marginally comfortable on the backseat. I was asleep in minutes.

I would have liked to have woken up after one or two dreamborn epiphanies, but instead, several hours later, the blare of an eighteen-wheeler jolted me awake. The car was stifling and I was sweating. My head was thick with sleep and no amount of thinking seemed to have a point.

I peed, drank water, had another candy bar and an orange and hit the road again. I knew I needed protein or I'd never clear my head, but I wanted to get a few more hours on the road before I stopped for the night. I was more than halfway to Baltimore. I still felt no eagerness at all to get there but damned if I wouldn't arrive, and in time.

I wasn't sleepy when I got to Weldon, ninety minutes shy of the Virginia border, but I was tired. Tired enough to know my reflexes were waning and I needed a decent meal and extended sleep. It was after six and I was afraid if I drove on, the cheap but decent motels would fill up. It would be nice to have some chicken, veggies, and maybe even a glass of wine along with it. If I left at an early hour in the morning, I would be in Baltimore by noon. That would leave an hour of family reunion before the funeral.

I didn't realize until I opened the car door that the air had changed. Inside, the car smelled like Florida, but outside it was cooler, fresher. There was a reason why people loved the Carolinas and Virginia, I thought. The landscape rolled with hills that parted to show off well-tended farms and red barns. Low-rising mountains, thick with green, broke the faraway views. I knew in June the humidity would be as bad as Florida's was year-round, but in April I found it more than bearable. If anything, I'd wish I had a sweater after dark.

The motel room cost more than I had hoped, but was not as expensive as I had dreaded. The room was very clean, which was my priority. Nothing skittered when I turned on a light in the bathroom.

Showered and refreshed, I drove the length of town to view my choices and decided on a chain restaurant that specialized in after-work happy hours and fried appetizers with cute names. I was in the mood for a fried appetizer with a cute name. I hadn't eaten away from the resort in weeks and weeks.

After my wine arrived, and I'd ordered, I wished that I had thought to bring a book. I hadn't packed any and wasn't likely to find something I'd like in the mega-store at the interstate strip mall. I'd go browse though. I'd get a book, open the cover and do what I'd done countless times: drop off to sleep by the end of the first paragraph.

I drank the wine a little too quickly and felt slightly loopy. My dinner looked good when it arrived—a platter of chicken breast skewers paired with spinach and mushrooms rolled into tortillas. I ripped into the chicken, feeling better just knowing I'd soon have protein in my bloodstream. The rolled thingies were tasty, too. I was nearly done when a voice behind me almost made me choke.

"Maybe you need another glass of wine to wash that down?"

I reluctantly looked up at the tall, black-haired guy. I knew he'd have a God's-gift smile even before I saw it. Good-looking, yes, I suppose. I felt like I knew his type—they were at the resort every week. At the resort I was certain of my coworkers' protection.

"I'm fine, thank you. I don't need anything."

"Sure?" He moved like he was going to sit down in the booth across from me, so I held up a hand.

"I am absolutely certain."

"Oh, come on—just a friendly drink."

"Really, I'm certain."

"You probably think I'm hitting on you, don't you?" He didn't say *bitch* but it was in his eyes. What is it with men that they don't think I can see that in their eyes even before I say no? The charm was all a façade. I was a bitch the moment I walked in the door and his dick twitched. The only difference was he was willing to withhold his opinion of me until after he'd seduced me. If I said yes, I would still be a bitch, with the addition of slut. I'd rather be just a bitch.

I wasn't at work. I didn't have to be diplomatic. I was also no wilting female trained to do anything to avoid being embarrassed in public. I glanced at his hand and said, "It doesn't matter what I think, but I'm sure it matters to your wife."

He said it and turned his back.

That is, until I said, very loudly, "Excuse me? What did you call me?"

Heads turned, and he didn't want that. My server came into view, looking like he'd seen this scene so many times it held absolutely no surprise.

Baltimore was in the South, unquestionably, but it wasn't the Deep South. Still, I was acquainted with the various buttons I could push on Southern men, and in this situation it didn't pain me at all to bat my eyelashes, look helpless and say, again very loudly, "This *married* man just called me a *rude* name because I refused a drink."

"She completely misunderstood."

"Perhaps you'd like to return to the bar," the server suggested to God's Gift. Unfortunately, the waiter was too bored to be convincingly unctuous.

The massive, broad-shouldered man at the next table, with off-duty cop written all over him, cleared his throat meaningfully. It was too much attention for God's Gift, who stalked back toward the bar, cursing under his breath. I heard the bartender offer him a free drink. I understood the tactic—nobody wanted to call the police, it was bad for business. But it wasn't right.

My server, ineffectively checking that I was okay, got the brunt of my anger.

"No, really, I'm not okay. He harasses me, calls me a rude

name, and then gets a free drink? Where's his incentive to be respectful toward your female patrons?"

The manager scurried over. I realized that in his mind, I was now the troublemaker because I wasn't going to laugh it off. "Ma'am, I'd be happy to comp your meal because of the unpleasantness. You've got apple cobbler on order, I see. Should that be brought out now?"

"No, thank you. I would like to leave. I realize you're not responsible for that man's behavior, but I don't feel safe anymore. In a half-hour he's going to hit on someone else, but I'm going to be upset about this all night. That's what's not fair."

"I understand, ma'am." Maybe he did. Some guys do get it. "If you will wait just a moment, I'll have the cobbler put in a box to go and I'll walk you to your car. I really am sorry about all this."

Mollified, I accepted his offer and he did, indeed, walk me to my car. As I drove away I thought he must have daughters or something, but that made me think that my own father wouldn't have done the same. He'd have said I got what I deserved, dining unescorted in an establishment that served alcohol.

Simmering with anger at how rotten men could be and how confusing it was that some of them weren't rotten at all, but mostly at my father's attitude that championed "boys will be boys," I went to the bookstore to walk the long aisles. The motion soothed me, as did the natural quiet of the store.

There were purportedly miles of books, but no gay/lesbian section I could find, even after walking every foot of the store.

Not wanting to ask right out—and risk getting stoned—I inquired at the desk if the store had a women's studies section.

"Oh, sure, honey," the clerk cheerfully told me. "Aisle ten, halfway down. We've got quite a few."

Perhaps I ought to have asked for "feminist books" because aisle ten, halfway down, was full of cookbooks, crafting manuals and lots of texts on the theory of home decorating. Maybe it also passed as their gay section; many of the books were written by openly gay men. Life was funny these days.

I turned the corner to find aisle eleven occupied with religious studies that continued on aisle twelve. I thought with great longing of the nice women's bookstore I'd found on a rare trip to Tampa with Tess. Finally somewhat satisfied with a mainstream mystery featuring a lesbian detective—though I doubted the bookstore knew that—I headed back to my motel. Once there I bolted the door, turned the air conditioner on high, kicked back on the bed wearing just an old T-shirt and ate the apple cobbler.

I lost myself in the book for a little while. Tess would be doing kid skit night right now. I liked kid skit night, it was fun.

There was a reason I'd left my father's world, and feeling trapped in a hotel room after dark was one of them. Used to walking around the resort at any hour of the day or night, I'd forgotten what the real world was like. Sure, I got hit on every week at the resort, but it was rare that the guy actually said what he was thinking. Some guys did actually take no with grace. Tess had had a few run-ins, but then Tess was so much more attractive than I was, and it brought out even more machismo and possessiveness in men.

Was Tess flirting with someone now? Was she thinking about me? I wanted to call her, but I worried she'd think I was checking up on her in some way if I called when she ought to be in her room. If she wasn't alone I didn't want to know. If she wasn't there, I didn't want to know.

I decided to leave her a message while she was still busy at skit night. To my horror, my voice quavered throughout. "I'm safe in North Carolina. I'll get there in plenty of time." Afraid the machine would hang up if I stopped talking, I quickly added, "I miss you. I'm sorry I had to leave."

I sat there with my hand on the phone for a very long time. I wanted to call back and explain that I was confused and more than missing her. I felt bereft not to have had dinner with her, not to have crossed paths with her a dozen times or more that day. She was a constant part of my life, and a good, caring friend. She kept her psychic accounts balanced, not just with me, but with everybody.

A kindness done her was returned, considerate gestures always answered. She remembered birthdays and asked after the health of parents and offspring. If she borrowed my golf clubs she always offered her car or something else to keep us even. If I made brownies she'd make cookies. I'd had college roommates who presumed my job in life was to share everything I had. Tess presumed nothing. Something about her brought out the kindness in others. She was, I thought, the first truly gentle person I had ever known. How could I call her and say that?

I closed my eyes and heard her voice. "So, you like to be teased." A thrill went through me, like it always did.

But I also heard her saying, "Can I get you more water while I'm up?" and "I have to wash my undies—want me to throw yours in too?" When I'd told her about the time my father had thrown a bundle of pipe at me with no warning, and then laughed when I dropped it, she'd said, passionately, "I'd give anything to have a dad, but not if he's anything like yours!" When I'd added that three days had gone by before either of my parents believed that my attempt to fend off the pipe had broken a finger, Tess had pulled me into a fierce hug and said in my ear, "No one should ever be cruel to you. I don't understand how anyone could."

She filled me with tenderness in places that weren't about sex. The parts of me that were all about sex she filled, too.

In that fog of impending sleep, I thought that I would give up all the Celine Griffins for Tess to actually be there with me. She gave me something no one else could. And that something was better than sex with other people.

Every time I woke in the night I felt her body under my hand.

Chapter Seven

Slamming car doors finally intruded and I woke to the gray light of early morning. Another day without Morning Stretch. I went through a routine anyway, not wanting to lose any of my flexibility. Of all of the aspects of my fitness, flexibility was the hardest for me to maintain.

Breakfast was mighty fine with real cornbread, eggs and fried country ham. It was more cholesterol than I'd normally eat in a full day, but I needed fortification to drive up to my old home and get out of the car. After breakfast I dressed for the services. There is no way that anyone can look good in basic black under the harsh light of a cheap motel bathroom. I looked like the services were for me.

Only the leather jacket would say that I was not what anyone assumed I was. Why didn't I have a row of piercings along one ear? A tongue stud, I thought. A tongue stud would make Aunt

Letty faint. Ask me to say a few words and I'd just whip that sucker out a couple of times.

I jammed my unused makeup back in the suitcase and headed for the car. The car started, even though I hoped it wouldn't. I drove toward the house where I had grown up, hoping for some sort of intervention.

Driving around or through D.C. was always a nightmare. Perhaps the town would be shut down for some sort of march, even on a Tuesday. Perhaps arrivals or departures of dignitaries would require lengthy, well-publicized delays. I could miss the funeral altogether and have an excuse to show.

I took the Innerloop and hit traffic near Silver Spring. The last I'd ever heard from Susan Porkland, who had kissed like a demon and enjoyed inept groping as much as I had, was a Christmas card postmarked Silver Spring. That had been four, maybe five, years ago. I knew our mothers had at one time been friendly. I wondered if I'd see Susan, and what she might be doing with her life.

I had to smile as I recalled the junior class field trip to the Washington Mall. Susan and I had snuck into every bathroom we'd passed, making out until we thought we'd be missed. That night, in the backseat of her parents' car, I had climaxed with someone else for the first time in my life. Now that I thought about it, Susan had teased me all day. Maybe that had set me up to like the anticipation of sex nearly as much as the orgasm. I should look her up and thank her, I thought.

When D.C. was behind me I knew it was only an hour to the moment of truth. Until the call on Monday afternoon, my mother's last words to me had been, "You've killed me and your father, just killed us. I hope you're happy!"

I was happy, I wanted to say. I felt all the anger again, that I wouldn't be able to tell my father that I knew he'd been fucking his secretaries. Mr. Pillar-of-the-Community, Mr. Sanctimonious-God-Hates-Queers, committed adultery with women on his payroll. Seemed like he was breaking a few Commandments there. But then, the people who were convinced they were the chosen ones always seemed to have a knack for picking and choosing the rules they'd abide by. Of course they insisted the rest of us live by all of the rules.

Baltimore's Little Italy was hit and miss in real estate. Some blocks were too close to the waterfront, others cozied up to a country club. My parents' little house was on a nice street, and the neighborhood hadn't changed much. Lawns were neatly mown and flowerbeds showed early signs of blossoms. The tupelos were dark with their waxy early spring leaves, and I remembered glorious fall afternoons where the streets were lined in their scarlet beauty.

Cars tended to be American-made late models or well-tended classics. It was the kind of neighborhood where a walk down the street told you what dinner was planned in each house, and the presence of a playset in the front indicated whether there were kids or not.

Uncle Bert's Town Car was parked in the driveway of my old house, and the narrow street was parked up. It seemed all too fitting that I had to park a block over and trail up the steps like a distant relative. I'd go in the freakin' front door, I thought. No back door for me. I wasn't really welcome, only tolerated.

I rang the bell, waited, then rang it again to get somebody's attention. The babble inside was loud, and that was just immediate family. After the services the house would be packed, a regular party. Maybe I'd park the Geo on the lawn, slap Pink in the CD player and get the party started.

Right.

"Brandy, darlin', how you've grown!" Aunt Dot opened the screen and gave me a not-quite hug.

"I've been this size for quite some time." My tone, I feared,

134

did not sound all that jovial. I thought again of having a tongue stud and had to suppress a near-hysterical giggle.

She glanced at my black slacks but held back the sigh I knew was there. She was my mother's youngest sister but every bit the stickler for propriety, for other people's kids at least. Her daughter, my cousin Judy, was a "gifted" artist and had always been allowed to dress, talk, walk, breathe and fuck whomever she wanted. What's a mother to do, Aunt Dot had worried aloud, with an *artistic* child? As if Judy had some sort of disease.

When I went over to their house for dinner, somehow I was the one who helped set the table and did the dishes, and was told to sit up straight. Judy drew pictures that were downright pornographic, if you asked me, but as long as every so often she cranked out a luminous Virgin Mary she could do as she liked.

Somewhere in a box I had one of her dirty drawings. For a long time I had wanted to be Judy and live at Judy's house. Then I'd seen Uncle Bert drunk at a wedding and realized we were both not exactly blessed in our parents.

The parlor was picture perfect. Waxy calla lilies flanked the settee with funereal stiffness. My mother was dabbing her eyes with a lacy white kerchief that contrasted starkly with her black dress and jacket. To either side sat my two older aunts, Emily and Letty. Each patted one of Mom's hands, and each looked pained to be thinking how their poor sister Irene would manage without her dear, devoted Wally.

I waited to be noticed. Nobody would speak to me until my mother did. I was damned if I was going to speak first.

I didn't have to wait long. My mother looked up and spread her arms with a long, drawn out, "Oh, Brandy! I was so afraid you wouldn't get here in time!"

"I got here as soon as I could." I was damned if I'd cry, though the room was so laden with heavy emotions it was hard not to respond to it.

My aunts cleared out, and I found myself in charge of the hand-holding and patting.

"How was your trip? Where are you staying? Do you have to hurry back?"

"Fine. I decided to drive. Air tickets were so much more expensive, and they wanted me to fly through Dallas to get here."

The detail was distraction enough. Uncle Bert promptly dominated the conversation with, "The airline industry constantly has its hand out to Uncle Sam, but they don't know how to run their business. It's corporate welfare, I tell you!"

"The last time Emily and I went down to Boca, we had to stop in Atlanta," Uncle Mike contributed. "That airport is a disgrace. We couldn't find a place to sit near the televisions and when we did the news was full of murders and bombings and queers getting married. It was disgusting."

Uncle Sal had something to add, but I tuned it out. My stomach was threatening to turn over as I choked with a flood of incoherent rage. I had wanted to stay away from this place and, in particular, these men. They talked loud and long, yielding the floor only to one another. They read the same newspaper, listened to the same radio shows. They treated their wives with a hostile affection that made Archie Bunker seem like a New Age Sensitive Guy. Was it any wonder I was a dyke? What kind of alternative did the likes of them give me?

Under the flow of the important, all-male conversation, my mother asked me again, "Where are you staying? Do you have to hurry back?"

I had thought I would stay here, I wanted to say, but the price wasn't worth the horrible churning going on inside me. I wanted out, away. I wanted to be free. How could they still get to me? I felt like a scared eight-year-old and I *hated* the feeling.

"I need to head back as soon as possible. The official policy is three days." It wasn't a lie, exactly.

My mother nodded and I realized that my answer wasn't unwelcome. I was here to complete the picture, nothing more. "That's a shame. You'll make it back if you leave this evening, won't you? But the roads are good, aren't they?"

"Yes, Mother, the roads are good." I patted.

The doorbell rang and my mother said hopefully, "That'll be Roger, I expect."

My stomach churned again when Roger came into the parlor. He looked more like my father than ever, including the little pig eyes that swept over me as if I was slop even he wouldn't touch.

My mother flew from the settee to my brother's bracing hug. "I don't know how I'll manage everything—"

"Don't you worry about anything, Mom. I've got it all covered. You just sit down and rest."

"Hello, Roger." I had escaped the settee as well. I wanted to keep going and escape the whole neighborhood.

"Glad you turned up."

Well, there was nothing more to be said, so I went to the kitchen for a glass of water. The counters and table were already groaning with food. On the vague hope they'd settle my stomach, I swiped two Wheat Thins from a platter of cheese and crackers. How could I have forgotten that being in this house made me feel this way?

When I went back to the parlor, there was an expectant hush.

"Irene," Aunt Emily said gravely, "we'd probably best be heading to the church."

As if magic incantations had taken root, everyone launched into action. Uncle Bert went to warm up the Town Car. The flowers were moved carefully to Uncle Sal's Regal while Roger himself escorted my ailing mother after Uncle Bert. I hoped to be forgotten, but after she was seated in the back she said in a loud voice, "Where's Brandy?"

Without answering, I went around to the door where Roger was waiting. He opened it for me a split second before I reached for it. I got in and barely had my feet clear before he slammed the door.

I started to swear at him, but I saw the look in his eyes. He'd meant to startle me, every bit the bully my father had been.

Nobody said a word the entire drive to the church. My mother didn't seem to require anything from me. I thought about Tess, about how alive she was, and I missed her with every beat of my heart.

As we pulled up to the door of Christ the Nazarene, my mother opened her handbag. "I knew you would need this."

I took the tiny hat—two bits of lace with some bobby pins to hold it on. It wasn't that the church required it, it was just the tradition of the ladies in the auxiliary, and every generation fell in line. I reflexively lifted it to my head, then stopped myself. I took a deep, steadying breath. "I'm not a member of this church, so it's hypocritical of me to wear this, Mother."

"Don't embarrass me this way."

"I will do my best, but I'm not wearing a lie."

My brother snapped, "Just wear the damn hat, Brandy!"

"You wear it, Roger, if it's so important to you."

My mother got out of the car with a flounce. Leaving the hat on the seat, I followed her before Roger could help me in any painful way. Up the steps we went, one big, happy family.

❧

I didn't listen to the service. I think if I had tried to listen I would have found it impossible not to cry or rant. I couldn't bring myself to look at the casket and I certainly wasn't going to walk past it at any point. Reverend Carter hadn't changed, and his voice flowed right past my ears, never entering.

I stood when it was time to sing, then sat again, staring down at my shoes. There was nothing anyone could say that would change my opinion of my father. He was a bully and a hypocrite. He condemned me for fucking women when he'd done plenty of that himself.

Elsewhere, I just wanted to be elsewhere, like on the beach at the resort, hunting for shells, or in a sunny garden of fragrant flowers, bees buzzing lazily while hummingbirds flitted from blossom to blossom. I would want Tess there with me and when I closed my eyes she was. Her body was curved over a flowerbed as she smoothed soil with her gloved hands. The light was soft and warm, and it seemed like a waste to spend another moment on anything as mundane as weeds.

I turned her face toward the light, then bent to kiss her sweetly, but with promising heat. I knelt next to her in the soft grass so I could take her into my arms.

Our bodies were suffused with the golden light that seemed to radiate from her eyes and smile. We were falling together, mouths feathering kisses on any skin we could reach. Touching her *anywhere* felt like touching sunshine. Her shoulders were as warm as her mouth and we were in danger of losing our edges, our form, as we melted together.

I bared her body and let the sun kiss her, too. The moon had seen us before, but not the sun, and I wanted to love her in all this light. Her rising nipples were peach in the daylight, and the flush of her arousal rinsed her face and neck with rose. I hovered over her like a hummingbird, taking sweetness wherever I found it, from her mouth, the hollow of her throat, the tawny concave of her stomach.

A light breeze stirred the air that enclosed us, and cherry blossoms drifted into her hair. She was as beautiful as fairy folk might be. That she let me hold her seemed to me to be a blessing beyond price.

And I knew that I would love her for as long as she would let me. I would know more and better love with her in a fantasy than my father had ever experienced in any real-life encounter.

I loved women, and he did not, and maybe that was all the difference between us I needed to understand.

I had escaped, I realized. I was not him, and would not ever turn into him. Whatever frustrations my life would bring I wouldn't take it out on anyone, certainly not anyone who couldn't hit me back.

I didn't belong in this dark church, or that airless parlor, or the Town Car or on the receiving end of one of Roger's petty little cruelties. Let Roger turn into our father. I pitied his kids, if he ever had any. I had loving arms to go home to, and home was where Tess was.

If she would have me.

I didn't even know what I would ask of her, or what I could promise, but that I wanted to ask meant something.

Throughout the rest of the service I felt like a ghost whose only power was to take up space and create a zone of silence. Were it not for my mother's talon-tight grip on my arm I would have left the church with everyone else, but instead I stood next to her, accepting condolences and inviting people back to the house.

"Oh, yes, so sudden, yes . . . what a shame . . . please drop by, no, nothing needed . . . so sudden . . . " I just kept murmuring the same words, over and over. Nobody knew me here. They never had.

Back in the Town Car, which seemed so small now, we set out at snail's pace behind the hearse, a long line of vehicles with orange FUNERAL placards in our front windows. When I got out of the car and smelled the fresh aroma of cut grass for a moment I forgot it was a cemetery. It was alive, and growing. Life, a little subdued to be sure, but life. Bees quietly went about their work while we walked, with great solemnity, to the graveside.

I managed to yield my place to Aunt Letty and moved carefully to the position farthest from the coffin yet not completely out of the grouping. I didn't want to be noticed. Words were muttered, my mother sobbed, and I wanted to be in my own home, with light and color, music and love.

What was I supposed to feel? My father had said his father smacked him around daily, was a hardass, rode him till the day he died. I suppose I was lucky. He hadn't hit me that often, and I'd been able to escape the riding for the last few years. I'd gotten a college education, too, more than my father had ever had. I didn't have to convince anybody to buy plumbing supplies or the latest line of kids' clothes. I didn't have to live his life. All right, maybe his life hadn't been so great. But I wasn't cutting him any slack. He fed me, clothed me, and never let me forget I was a burden.

Standing there I recalled for the first time in years overhearing him argue with my mother about the cost of Tampax. The bargain brand was cheaper, he'd insisted. I wished I'd had the courage then to do what I had wanted, which was to tell him to shove both brands up his ass and tell me he couldn't feel the difference.

Roger had Levi's and I had Kmart generic. He went out for basketball; I stayed in for ironing. He got paid ten bucks a C and I got five bucks an A. It's just the way it was. If I ever have kids, it won't be that way.

Did Tess want kids? Had she thought about it? Where we lived wasn't exactly conducive to maternity, nor was a job that ran ten hours a day nearly seven days a week.

You're standing in a cemetery, thinking about babies, Brandy. You're flipping your lid. I stifled a chuckle. First time in ages I wanted a joint. I didn't know where I was staying tonight, but part of my evening plan was coconut milk, ice and a bottle of spiced rum.

More handshakes and condolences. I was popular today as long as the conversation was short and ended with a firm good-bye.

Cousin Judy, wearing red—but what do you expect of an artist—actually hugged me. "I'm really sorry this is what brought you home."

"Wish I'd worn red," I said in her ear.

"You'd be surprised what you can get away with when you just can't help yourself." She widened her eyes dramatically after our hug ended.

"Anything but being queer," I said under my breath.

She laughed. "You capped your career with that one. I'll never forget the day you outran the entire boys' track team."

I grinned. It was a crowning achievement to a track career for which I'd had to buy my own running shoes when Roger walked around every day in Reeboks, courtesy of Dad. "I guess it's okay to fuck them, but you can't outrun them."

There was a little gasp from the nearest relative, but Judy's resounding laugh covered my f-word outrage. "Even if outrunning them is the only way to get out of fucking them, huh?"

I could hang with Judy, I decided. "Please say you're coming back to the house. I know how to unlock the liquor cabinet."

"I'd like to, but I have to pick up my kids at school. My day to carpool. I really do have to bolt to get there in time. Drop me some news from time to time, okay? Judy at JudyArt-dot-com."

Kids? Judy had kids? When had that happened? I watched her red clogs high-tailing it toward a Saturn station wagon. Judy was still a breath of fresh air, but even she had changed.

Drifting away from the platitudes and discussions of God's will, I realized I was staring at Susan Porkland. Susan Porkland of the hot lips and hot hands, and who was not too shy to put her mouth "down there."

She was in the line of people slowly walking by my mother. I didn't think she'd been at the church, but then I hadn't looked at anybody.

She caught me staring. I grinned across the distance separating us and would have walked the few steps to say hello except that she turned her back on me and pointedly took the arm of the man next to her. I knew her brothers, and he wasn't any of them. So, hubby or boyfriend, I had to presume.

She actually turned her back on me. On *me*, the girl who'd also not been too shy to put her mouth "down there." The girl she'd read porn to and shoplifted beer with. The girl who fucked her, and she loved to fuck. Was Susan just another straight girl who'd decided sex with girls was safer and easier until she grew up?

I stared at her back and wanted to say, "You can tense that tight ass all you want, Susie-Q, but that doesn't mean it didn't happen." I wanted to chase after the man she was with and say, "Did you know she loves to suck pussy?"

I was starting to think I was the only lesbian I'd ever slept with.

Well, there was Celine Griffin, and Celine had been mighty fine in bed. But no, that wasn't good enough for me anymore. No fan-fucking-tastic romps in bed with women who loved women. No, I had to be in love with Tess, who was wonderful

143

and kind and fine and smart and funny and sexy and lovely and might not be ready to be a woman-lovin'-woman one hundred percent of the time.

I watched Susan Porkland drive away. Which life was the lie? The frantic hours with me and the other girls I knew about? Or the one she was going to?

Another silent Town Car ride. Uncle Bert was a fine chauffeur.

Roger glanced over the seat at my mother. "I ordered an extra set of death certificates for the insurance company."

"I'm sure they'll be necessary." My mother sniffed into her handkerchief.

I finally asked the only thing I wanted to know. "What was the official cause of death? Stroke?"

Roger snapped back, "What do you care?"

"Don't squabble," my mother said automatically, giving me the evil eye.

"All I did was ask how my father died. I think I have a right to know."

"Don't shout, Brandy."

I hadn't even raised my voice. "When I'm shouting you'll know, believe me."

My mother sighed heavily and I kicked myself for letting her goad me into sounding like a teenager. "It was a stroke. Blood clot in the brain. He wouldn't stop salting his food, and all those years driving from one town to the next, eating diner food."

And boinking anything he could afford, I added silently.

Roger helped Mom out of the car, then Uncle Bert took over. I found my way blocked by my brother, who was up on the balls of his feet exactly the way our father had stood when he had something to say and all nearby needed to pay heed. "He had a will and he left it all to Mom. And Mom's left it all to me. So there's no point you being here trying to suck up."

"Fine, whatever. I don't want anything. You can keep the Hummels and the *Playboy* magazines in the basement."

He sneered. "You liked to look at them well enough."

"Yeah. Like father, like daughter. He liked to fuck women and so do I."

"Don't talk about Mom like that!" He leaned into my space, just letting me know I was within reach of a punch.

"Who says I'm talking about Mom? I'm talking about Monica and Marilyn and Tina. I can't tell you how great it was to walk in on him and Cathy. And there's no telling who he did on his sales trips."

"You have such a filthy mind, you always were a perv."

"What about you, Roger? Not married yet?" With a sudden insight, I realized something I ought to have figured out long ago. "You don't want the *Playboys*, though, do you? You never liked to look."

"What's that supposed to mean?"

I shrugged. "At least I'm honest about who I like to fuck."

"Leviticus, perv. Choke on it."

"Is that what you do?"

Roger cocked his arm back and I knew if I moved he'd hit me. "Shut your fucking filthy mouth, Brandy, or I'll shut it for you."

I said nothing, did nothing, just stared.

"Queer," he snapped. With that towering insult, my brother stalked toward the house.

"When you stop hating yourself, call me," I yelled after him. I wanted to tell him all the things he'd said to me. If our mother would go to an early grave because of her dyke daughter, how would she fare knowing she had a queer son? I knew if I said it he would hit me, but that wasn't what kept my mouth shut. Someday, maybe, he wouldn't hate himself so much, and I couldn't bring myself to do anything that would slow that day's arrival.

I was still standing on the steps when the neighbor, Mrs. Salinski, paused to offer me condolences and an oatmeal-chocolate chip cookie. I accepted both.

It was a nice day. Outside the air was fresh and there was sunshine.

I realized I hadn't worn that stupid hat into church and the world hadn't come to an end.

Mom had never been mean like Dad, but her weapons had been more subtle. I didn't exist for her right now, and maybe I never would. I might check back every five years, just to see if she cared. She had Roger to dote on her, and that's who she wanted. Trying to get anything else from her would just frustrate both of us.

I didn't have to wear the damn hat.

And I didn't have to go into the house now. I didn't have to endure anything I didn't choose. I was as free as I chose to be.

One block over I got into my Geo. Pointing it south I thought if I pushed I might be on the other side of D.C. before rush hour got really bad.

Okay, I was wrong about rush hour in D.C. I expected *Air Force One* to do a flyover or something, traffic was so bad. After a half-hour spent creeping toward the closest off-ramp, I headed into a part of the District I wasn't familiar with. To my relief, I found a crowded diner with a couple of cop cars out front. Though the area of town was dicey, it was probably safe with the uniforms swilling coffee at the counter. I joined them and they never noticed me. Nobody noticed me except the waitress, who brought me a nice plate of fatty pot roast, real mashed potatoes and vegetables that had been boiled for a couple of hours, then salted.

The milkshake, like the potatoes, was real all the way

through. I watched the waitress fill the tall silver tin with whole milk, chocolate ice cream, chocolate syrup and a spoonful of malt. I watched it the whole time it was hooked on the blender. A few minutes later she filled a glass with half the contents and left the rest of the frosty tin to tempt me.

After my queasiness of the morning it was one of the best meals I'd had in years. The knots in my stomach eased, and the headache edging around my eyes evaporated. I was free and I was starting to believe it.

I wanted to drive all night and get home, home to Tess, as soon as possible. Every minute away felt like I was losing her. Traffic would be against me. My own body, now drooping with reaction from the long drive and high stress, was against me.

My own heart began to argue against itself. *Go home to Tess*, it said one moment, then the next it was *go play all night at Dupont Circle*. Find a bar, get laid, really be free. *You've spent too much time in your head. Dump it all and go to bed.*

But the other part of my heart warned me not to confuse freedom with license to be stupid. I'd done that in college, and I'd regretted it ever since. I wasn't the kind of person who got to go through life lucky and dumb.

I mopped up the last of the pot roast gravy with the last of the biscuit and turned my attention to finishing the milkshake. My cousin Judy had kids and a station wagon, but she did seem as full of zest as ever. That quick glance at Susan Porkland's withdrawn face, though, hadn't spoken of a happy life. We'd all changed and were changing.

I hadn't worked out in more than forty-eight hours and I could feel lethargy and a growing desire for Goo Goo Clusters and Moon Pies, by the case. I had just gobbled down an entire meal of comfort food and I wanted more. Okay, so I was still angry at my father, and pissed off at my brother, and just plain hurt that my mother hadn't wanted any part of me except the

Dutiful Daughter. I had shown up, hadn't I? Even knowing what my reception would be like, I'd gotten there in time.

Tess, I thought, would talk me through this. But I didn't want to throw myself on Tess's couch in an impromptu therapy session. I wanted to be on her couch only if she was on me. Remembering the way she had tasted, the way she had moved when I devoured her, left me shivering. I wanted it all: the talk, the laughter *and* the great sex. All of it, with the same woman.

Traffic was still wretched when I left, though I had dallied as long as I could. Trips down various promising boulevards didn't bring me to any shopping malls where I could kill a few hours. I made my way toward the Potomac, but ultimately, if you want to cross the river you have to use a bridge. The Clara Barton Parkway inched along. The sun was low in the sky before I was on the other side.

Virginia had become a gigantic parking lot. By eight o'clock I was seeing double and ready to scream from the noise in my head and the frustration of stop-and-go traffic. I wanted to pummel something, forget it all, have Tess and stay footloose. I headed toward a cluster of motels. Then I did what any sensible, ready-to-grow-up dyke would do. I booked a room for the night, and, courtesy of a nearby liquor store, I found my way to the bottom of a bottle of rum.

Chapter Eight

I didn't remember how I fell asleep. I'll always remember how I woke up, though, which was throwing up everything I'd eaten for the last five years.

I don't recall ever being that sick from alcohol, but then again, I'd never downed a fifth of rum over the course of several hours. The first third of the bottle had turned me into the sex goddess of all time, and I'd sprawled across the bed in all my naked glory, seducing and satisfying one woman after another, and not always one at a time.

Somewhere in the middle third of the bottle I had solved the national debt, cured homophobia, and had Tess on my lap, promising to be mine.

The problem with my alcohol-induced brilliance was that the last third of the bottle had obliterated it all. I had kept drinking because I could feel every time he'd hit me.

"You were born stupid . . . you'll never get it . . . Don't think, you'll just screw it up . . . You might run fast but you can't catch worth shit . . . No man will ever want you for more than an hour . . . You're useless . . . Tramp . . . worthless . . . pervert."

Every memory of his voice played over in my mind and I toasted it, over and over, until the only thing I could say for certain was that I had outlived him. Of course in the morning, whether I'd outlive him for long seemed uncertain.

Worshipping the porcelain god for several hours did not do my soul a bit of good. It wasn't sexy, it wasn't smart. It wasn't a rite of passage, even. Just because I felt misunderstood didn't make me a rock star.

I was a pretty ordinary girl from an unremarkable place. I had an outrageous name, I loved women, and when I asked my legs to run ten miles, they would. Nothing all that rare in me, and I didn't know what I could possibly offer to Tess. What had Celine Griffin seen in me beyond a great time in bed? I wasn't sure there was anything more to me than that.

When I finally checked out, a little after eleven, I got in my warm car and went to sleep, never leaving the motel parking lot.

The dashboard clock was broken, I decided. It had to be. It couldn't be five o'clock and I couldn't still be in Springfield, Virginia, possible home of the Simpsons—that is, if they had Southern accents.

Food was necessary, but I made a wise choice to go to a mall I'd passed just off the freeway. Soup and bread went down. After a few anxious moments, it thankfully stayed down.

What had possessed me to drink my way to oblivion? *So you're pissed at your father, Brandy*. Hurt him—that was now impossible. But hurting myself wasn't the next best thing. He won if I lost, and I was damned if I'd give him the satisfaction.

Maybe I was useless as the son he wished he'd had, but I was a woman, and I had use for myself. I touched the envelope of cash in my handbag and felt the warming comfort of knowing my life brushed against others' and we were better for it. I'd not heard anyone at the funeral say, "I'm a better person for Wally Monsoon being in my life."

If I succeeded at nothing else, it would be that. They would carve on my tombstone, "Life wouldn't have been nearly as good without her." It wasn't much of an aspiration but it was achievable. It was more than a great many people, it seemed to me, had ever managed. If I wasn't going to cure cancer or broker world peace, I could do far worse than being a good friend to as many people as possible.

I wanted Tess . . . she would understand all that I was thinking. She'd help me make even more sense of it. If Tess could understand how I was feeling then I'd know for sure I was figuring things out. Such a mix of anger and resolve and hurt and chagrin and . . . hope? Was that hope I felt? About what?

Almost feeling like a human being, I hit the road with every intention of driving nonstop all the way home. But within a few hours my vision was swimming and my temples were throbbing and I had to find another place to sleep. Florence, South Carolina, was a place I'd always wanted to visit, I told myself. Right. It was good-bye Thursday within moments of putting my spinning head onto the pillow.

I usually don't dream that I remember, so when I woke up Friday morning, I wasn't disappointed. My vision still felt like I was tracking slow. Inversions during any kind of stretching were out of the question, but I was going to live.

The nightstand clock said seven a.m. I visualized the map in the car and a slow smile crossed my face. If I left now I'd still make Celine Griffin's show. I'd missed out on Circus Night, my one early morning on the greens, admiring and flirting with dykes for several days, and—worst of all as my stomach growled—French oatmeal on Friday mornings, with vanilla sugar and dried diced mango.

Okay, so I couldn't do anything that put my head below my heart, but I lost myself in the gentle rhythm of unchallenging yoga. My right thigh told me it didn't want to do forward bends, but I coaxed it, relaxed, and let go.

I was letting go of other things, I could feel that. Sunrise, a new day, a new phase in life. Tonight I was going to see the woman I loved and the thought of that was the best drug I'd ever had. I didn't know if I'd have the courage to muddle my way through explaining all that I wanted. I hoped when I got there that I would know what to do.

Unlike the drive up, I was intensely aware of the landscape outside the car's confines. The rolling green woods gave up flocks of birds to the morning air. A smoky mist lifted from cotton fields nestled in the embrace of hills. The sky lightened with the passing hours until the blue was dusted over with tiny white puffs of cloud.

I left the rolling hills of the Carolinas to glide into the slow, easy landscape of Georgia. Nearing the Florida border I picked up some fruit and crackers in a minimarket where I also got gas, then followed the signs to a parking area overlooking a large waterfowl sanctuary.

The overlook didn't seem promising, but a lush, rolling beauty took my breath away. The wetlands were lovely. I wanted Tess to see the flock of glistening gulls, so white against the sky it hurt my eyes.

Was this what it would be like? The rest of my life, wishing she was there to share so much more than sex with me?

I know she liked me, but could she love me? Or would she be like Susan Porkland, and like the sex but go for a man when it was time to be real about life?

I wasn't going to be able to sleep, to breathe even, until I knew how she felt. I had laughed at people in movies and books who dithered about love and couldn't make a cup of tea because love was so painful and wonderful. So I had to laugh at myself. All I could do right now was point the car south and think about her.

I couldn't even see past the moment when I asked her how she felt. I wouldn't be alive until I had her answer.

I knew I was back in Florida when no music I brought with me was loud enough to compensate for the seemingly unchanging landscape. It was a relief to reach the strip malls of Orlando and drive by the Mickey Ears on I-4. I would get home by dinner. I'd have one last evening with all those great women, none of whom hated themselves for what they were. Most of whom were busy being grown-up and real. They made their families in their own image, and I wanted to be a lesbian with them. I wanted to feel normal again, what was normal for me.

I was in time to find the raisin nut cake still warm at the buffet. I'd parked the car and come directly to dinner, my stomach a growling knot. My arms and legs were trembling ever so slightly, from all the sitting and vibration, I thought. Several staff members welcomed me back, and I kept my eyes open for Tess.

Smoked salmon was wonderful on a bed of spring greens. The diner meal had been comforting, but this was home. Being away made me appreciate my good fortune to like my work and coworkers, and be in a position to decide if this week's smoked salmon was as good as last week's. I was welcomed at the table where other staffers were dining and assured everyone I was doing fine, as was my family. Why give them a downer at dinner?

There was no sign of Tess, however, but it was after seven and we always tended to eat earlier in the evening. Perhaps she was dressing up for a date. I did not want to think she was . . . otherwise occupied.

I was headed for the parking lot and my suitcase when I heard Celine calling my name. We exchanged a firm hug.

"Shouldn't you be sequestered away with preshow jitters or something?"

"Nah, I don't do that, though I will disappear for fifteen minutes or so. How was your trip?" Her yellow-ringed blue eyes searched mine.

"What I expected, mostly. I was there long enough to remember all the reasons I left. So I came back." Our arms were still around each other and I sighed into another embrace. It felt good to be held.

"I didn't think I'd see you again, and that would have been a shame."

"I wanted to see your show," I said, which was the truth. It just wasn't the only reason I had tried to make it back tonight. "I've been a big fan for a really long time."

She squinted one eye shut and gave me a sheepish look. "Don't go all fan on me. It was too real. If you were with me because I'm famous it'll break my heart."

I shook my head. "I was with you because you're sexy, appealing and smart. The second time because you're sexy, appealing, smart *and* a powerful, wonderful lover."

She cupped my face with a hand I remembered all too well on other parts of my body. Softly, she asked, "What about tonight?"

154

"I . . . I'm hoping to spend some time with my best friend."

"The blonde? Tess?"

"Yeah. I hope we can talk about a broader definition of best friend, actually."

"Oh, as in . . . ?" She gazed at me a moment, then said, "Still looking for forever?"

"I don't know if I'll find it. But looking could be a lot of fun."

She pulled me close for a moment. "If you ever go out looking in the wide world again, drop by. It's the damnedest thing that as soon as you left I kept thinking we never got a chance to talk about anything, and I think I would have liked that."

I shrugged and rested my head on her shoulder. The sticky night air didn't mask her intriguing cologne. "I think I would have, too. Let's agree to be wistful and say things like, 'We'll always have Florida.' "

She laughed as she let go of me. "Wistful. Yeah, it's how I'll remember you, Brandy Monsoon."

"You should go get ready, I think." I grinned at her as she took several side steps in the direction of her room.

"You're right. See you later, I hope."

"Break a leg," I called lightly.

"Brandy?" She was now on the other side of the reception area walkway. "I'll also remember your great ass."

I laughed and didn't mind that several people obviously overheard. I retrieved my suitcase and rolled it happily to my quarters.

From the moment I unlocked the door I knew something was different. The aroma was different—pine-scented cleanser, very faint. Once I was all the way in I realized I wasn't smelling my laundry pile or the ubiquitous musty mildew aroma of damp corners. Tess had done my laundry and scrubbed down the kitchen. The bed was made and turned down. It even looked like there might be clean sheets.

What a sweet thing to do, I mused. It was so . . . her.

Leaving my suitcase to be unpacked later, I quickly rinsed off in the shower and reached for the little black dress I saved for special occasions. I added the high-cut lace panties that I hoped Tess would enjoy taking off of me later. That is, if I could convince her to come back to bed with me, if I found the courage to tell her how I felt and if she, well, liked hearing that.

My hair pulled back into a glittering hair tie Tess had given me for Christmas, I slipped into slinky black ballet flats and headed out the door.

Tess wasn't in the dining room or bar, nor did I spot her in the slow-moving crowd heading for the performance. It was chaotic in Village Square, with little people dashing about in face paint. I spotted Bleachie, but Tess wasn't anywhere near, which was a relief. I didn't think Tess would forgo the entertainment, so I slipped my way through the crowd to look inside.

The lights dimmed by half just as I took stock of the room. Tess wasn't immediately in sight, but she had to be there somewhere.

Moika was taking a seat near the back. I got her attention with a hand on her shoulder. "Have you seen Tess?"

"You're back!" She hopped up to hug me. "Yes, she was here a bit ago. Your family is well?"

"As well as can be expected," I answered noncommittally. The lights dropped another half. "Oh, darn it, they're starting."

"Maybe she's backstage," Moika suggested helpfully.

Of course, I thought. I excused myself and hurried along the side wall to the stage door. No way was I going up the center stage stairs in this outfit. Half the audience would see my ass, and I only wanted one woman admiring it tonight.

Maneuvering my way to the wings I caught sight of a tousle

of blonde hair. I paused, overcome with shyness. After a minute I managed a few little steps, hoping that Tess would finish what she was doing and turn around.

Randall began his announcements and usual stage patter.

Celine abruptly clattered up the stairs behind me. Before I could say a word, she let out a wolf whistle and pulled me into an embrace. "You could kill with that dress."

I was acutely aware that Tess had to have heard and was probably looking at us now. "You could kill with those jeans," I replied in kind, trying to extricate myself before Tess reached us.

"Thanks, darlin'. I meant what I said about your ass."

Blushing, I laughed. "Randall is just about to introduce you."

"Be down front for me?" She leaned into me for a smooch on the lips.

"In a bit, I think."

"And now the woman you've been waiting all week for," Randall boomed, "Celine Griffin!"

Celine closed her eyes, whispered something to herself, then whisked onstage with a brilliant smile.

I stared at Tess, not a word in my head that I could even articulate. She looked . . . great. Smelled great. She was wearing a clinging aqua jumpsuit that I knew from personal experience unzipped all the way down to her crotch. It clung to parts of her so suggestively that I wasn't sure she was wearing a stitch underneath it. Finally, I found my voice and produced a quiet, "Hi."

"I'm glad you're back safe," she said. "I thought you might make it back for tonight, though." Then she hugged me, hugged me the way Aunt Dot had hugged me, barely touching.

Celine's first comment drew a laugh.

"Thank you for everything you did at my place."

She shrugged. "When I woke up it seemed the least I could do. I had my own laundry."

157

"You changed the sheets."

She flushed and looked away. "I'm sure that will be welcome this evening."

"Yeah. After motels . . . "

Tess said something, but it was drowned out by another burst of laughter. In the following lull she said, "You're missing the show."

"I know." I let my eyes drink her in. She seemed distant, and I didn't know what to make of it. "Aren't you going to see it?"

"Sure. A couple of women invited me to sit with them."

"Oh. Okay."

Tess walked toward the stage door stairs.

"Tess? What's wrong?"

She turned briefly to face me. "Nothing," she lied, with a big fake smile on her face. "Be safe."

Stung by her unwillingness to talk about whatever was bothering her, I said, "Don't do anything I wouldn't do."

"Or anyone?"

What the heck had that meant?

I followed her into the audience and she sat down alongside someone I didn't know, but then again, I'd missed most of the chances to mingle with the ladies. I also found a seat. Paying attention to Celine was difficult, even though, judging by the howls of laughter, she was at the top of her form. When she came down the main stairs into the audience, it was easier to forget that Tess was sitting a few rows back.

"All you grownups come back later for another set, just for the over-eighteen crowd, if you follow, but I thought what I'd do now is ask some questions." She paused next to two women, each with a small child on her lap. Carefully, she got the nearest child to answer a few questions about his age and his moms' names.

"What does Mommy Bet do to make money? What's her job?"

From where I sat I saw the mother in question put her face in her hand as if she dreaded the answer.

The clear, piping voice answered, "She rents U-Hauls."

After the laughter died down, Celine said, "Never work with kids. They upstage you every time. What does Mommy Nina do?"

"She's a therapist."

"That's what I like," Celine quipped, "the convenience of one-stop shopping. Rent the U-Haul, proceed directly to therapy."

I laughed as heartily as anyone, but I still wasn't losing myself in the performance. I would have told anyone that one of my dreams was to see Celine Griffin live and all I could think about was Tess's being upset with me. I was bemused and distracted. Lovelorn, sunstruck, moonstruck, you name it. I thought about the night I left, how she had kissed me like a lover. Kissed me like she wanted to do it for hours. I wasn't living in a fantasy world; she had wanted me.

When Celine moved to the other side of the room I snuck over to the side aisle and slowly moved up a few rows.

"Tess," I hissed.

The woman nearest me gave me an irritated look.

"Tess!"

Tess turned her head in disbelief. I beckoned. She rolled her eyes. I beckoned again.

"I'm sorry," she muttered as she stepped over the irritated woman. "What?"

"Shh!" The irritated woman vented her annoyance. I took Tess by the arm, leading her to the back of the room, then into the deserted foyer beyond the rear doors.

Tess was looking at me as if I'd lost my mind. "What's wrong?"

"That's what I want to know. What's wrong? Why are you mad at me?"

"I'm not mad at you, Brandy. It's like being mad at the ocean for washing up too high on the sand."

I tried to work my way through that but got nowhere. "Something is wrong, though."

"I thought you wanted to see the show."

"I do, but not if you're upset with me." I wanted to say that she mattered too much for me to assume that later was good enough to talk to her. I wanted to ask her to kiss me again.

"I'm not upset with you."

"Then with something."

"This is pointless, Brandy. I would like to see the show, too. Now I know why you had her picture."

I flushed. "You remembered."

She nodded. "It's okay."

"I don't have a crush on her."

"I know." Her eyes were filled with sadness. "Randall got Barbados."

I blinked. "He did?"

"Yeah. He wants to take some of the fitness staff with him."

"Oh."

We stared at each other. I had no idea what she was thinking. Was she going to apply for it? Was there room for two, or did she want to get away from me? We'd made love, and that had been too much?

"So," she finally said. "That's that."

I didn't understand what she meant, and my mouth had disconnected from my brain. There were a million words spinning in my mind but not one would join with another to make any sense.

A burst of laughter startled us both.

"I really would like to see the show," Tess said.

Say something, my mind wailed.

She shrugged. "Okay then."

"Did you read the note I left?"

"Yeah." She turned to the door. "I obviously didn't get it."

She was gone before I could even voice my confusion. I didn't understand.

What's a girl to do? I escaped to the nearest ladies' room, where the mirror told me the dress looked great and the panties were visible enough to be criminal. Tess hadn't wanted me in this package. She hadn't seemed to even want to talk. I was a dumbshit. I couldn't be happy with her wonderful, supporting friendship. No, I had to want more.

Instead, I was losing both. Madeline had broken my heart in college, and it had hurt, but it hadn't felt like this. I'd been upset and angry, devastated even. But I'd accepted that of course I would survive it, because one survived such blows and went on to write bad poetry about it. Adversity built character, didn't it?

I looked at my frozen, pale face in the mirror, remembering that I had wished for what I felt inside—loving Tess, loving women—to show on the outside. It seemed like it showed tonight. I didn't recognize my mouth or the stricken look in my eyes.

I had stood there and said nothing. Our conversation had made no sense at all, and I had done nothing to change that. I stepped back and flexed my biceps. I was good with my body, but at words I sucked. I hadn't always been able to lift double my weight, however. It had taken practice, patience and fortitude. I didn't finish the first three marathons I started, but I did the fourth.

So, if Tess was worth having—and she was, I wanted to wail—I would have to work harder. I would have to try again.

I looked at myself in the mirror and said aloud, "I don't understand. Could you say that another way?" Right, I could be that calm. Sure.

Okay, fine, I told myself. What you're doing isn't working, so you have to change if you want her. Wrapping yourself up in a cute package is not the same as saying loud and clear, "I want to be with you. I want to walk a road with you, and see how long it goes."

Tomorrow, I thought.

I was fragile and frazzled. Tomorrow I would talk to Tess. Tomorrow I wouldn't be so afraid as to ask what opportunities in Barbados meant to her. I would try again tomorrow, and the day after, and the day after that.

The crowd was stomping and laughing when I headed for my quarters and bed. I was missing a live Celine Griffin performance, but maybe it wasn't so bad that I recognized what mattered more to me.

Chapter Nine

The night sky was bright with stars, but the moon hadn't yet risen. I loved the soothing sound of the surf and I wished not so much for the romantic picture of Tess and me strolling hand in hand on the beach, but for the reality of her hand in mine, wherever we walked.

I hung up the dress and dropped the panties in the empty laundry basket. Stark naked, I unpacked my suitcase. Most of my clothes smelled of rental car and stale motel rooms. Toiletries I put back in the bathroom, shampoo in the shower, shoes neatly under the closet shelving. I might as well try to keep the small space looking as tidy as Tess had left it.

Knowing I'd feel better after a long, hot shower, I started it running. My brain seemed content to replay every moment of my life with Tess, every glass of wine, every brownie, every laugh over a flubbed workout move, every high five after a routine that felt really good. We didn't get to watch much television, but there was always time for a little bit of talk, many times throughout any given day. My life was full of her but my heart seemed to ache with emptiness.

I stood under the needles of hot water for a while, just breathing in the steam. Shampoo and conditioner felt good, as did my favorite mango-scented body wash. I was still letting the conditioner soak in when I glimpsed something rounded and aqua through the fogged glass door.

"You scared the shit out of me!" I scrubbed furiously at the glass to see Tess better.

"Why aren't you fucking Celine tonight?"

"I don't want to fuck Celine tonight!"

"I thought she was your type!" Tess was just on the other side of the glass, her neck and shoulders flushed with red.

"She was. I thought men were your type!" The glass fogged and I smeared it again.

"I thought so too. I got over it."

We stared at each other through the glass. She said something, but I couldn't hear over the water. "What?"

"If you didn't want to see Celine's show, why did you rush back here and drape yourself all over her?"

I licked water off my lips and chose the easier question to answer. "I didn't drape myself all over her. I like her, and I needed a hug and I guess . . . we're sort of friends."

Tess put her hand on the glass. She was breathing hard. "Then why are you here, if it wasn't to get back in time to see her again?"

"This is home." I took a deep breath. Talking takes practice. "This is where you are."

"What?"

"Oh, fuck this," I snapped. I leaned back into the water to rinse the conditioner out of my hair. "Give me a minute."

164

I scrubbed furiously, in a strange place emotionally between irritation at having my shower interrupted, trepidation at having to talk to Tess so soon when I hadn't really thought through what I wanted to say, and the simple reality that I was naked in front of her and wet in more ways than one.

Emotions were raging through me, and they all wanted words. I had to find them or I didn't have a chance of any kind of life with Tess. Even if she didn't love me back, talking was the only shot I had at keeping her as a friend. I could not imagine life without her there.

The air in the shower changed and I blinked water out of my eyes. Tess had opened the door and her eyes were . . . devouring me. My heart skipped a beat.

"Close the door," I said automatically. "You'll slip on the wet floor in those shoes."

She kicked off the delicate sandals and stepped into the shower with me.

"Your . . . your jumpsuit, it'll get—"

"Did you say you hurried back because I was here?"

Yes, I tried to say. Yes was the right answer. I nodded.

She pulled the zipper of the jumpsuit down and it parted slowly to reveal nothing but skin. Water gathered on her chest, drops spilled between her breasts, and I wanted to chase them with my tongue. It was hard to swallow, even harder to think, but somewhere inside I remembered enough to know that another fabulous night of sex would be grand, but it was not a substitute for simple words like *yes* and *I love you*.

"You hurried back so we could go on being buddies? Fuck buddies?"

Yes, no. Well, I wasn't sure of the right answer. I hadn't thought about whether if we were lovers that meant we were no longer fuck buddies or best friends. Were some terms mutually exclusive? Why was this all so confusing?

Oh, for fuck's sake, Brandy, *talk*!

"I hurried back because I'm better here. Better here with you. I make more sense here with you. I feel more with you. I want . . . you."

She stopped unzipping just below her navel. "You can't blame hormones for everything."

Stung, I snapped back, "This isn't about hormones or needing a good roll in the sack. I had that with Celine." Okay, I hadn't meant to say that last part.

"I had it with Gloria," she asserted with a toss of her head.

"So why are you in my shower?"

"Are you in love with Celine?"

"No!"

"Are you going to apply for Barbados?"

"Only if you are. I won't go without you!"

Her eyes flashing, she accused, "You're in love with me!"

"Yes, I am! You got a problem with that?"

She kissed me with a hungry bite and we were both under the water. She cupped my ass, and my hips naturally curved into hers as my hands pushed the jumpsuit off her shoulders. Her face was wet, her shoulders warm, her breasts melting into mine. Hot and sweet, she was all that, and in the back of her throat I heard the moan I'd learned the first night we'd been together.

"Tess, Tess, wait . . . " It was nearly impossible to make my arms obey, but I pushed her gently away.

Her mouth looked bruised from kisses and I wanted to go back to rubbing my lips over hers. Looking dazed, she asked, "What?"

"Do you believe in forever?"

She took my chin between her fingers. "Not until you."

"Oh." Her answer was so perfect, so wonderfully Tess, romantic and sweet and everything like that, I didn't know how

I could possibly add to it. I took a deep breath, sucked in some water and had to cough. How suave.

She moved to kiss me again and I held her off. "What, Bran?"

I opened my mouth and then the words were there. "I have to say this or maybe I never will. It doesn't make any sense, but I've never felt like this before and I've never thought about how if you don't start a marathon you'll never know if you can finish. But a race has a finish line and forever doesn't, and how will you ever know if you get there? You can't know, not for certain. All you can do is run the race."

I stopped to wipe away tears I hoped she thought were from the shower.

Panting for air, I rushed on, "All you can do is run the race and love every minute of it and do everything you can to push that finish line so far away you can't ever see it, never get there, and you have to work, keep fit, keep listening to your body and your heart so you can go on running, walking, whatever it takes. That's what I want. As long as you're with me there. That's what I want."

I burst into tears she couldn't mistake and she held me very tight.

"That made perfect sense to me, Brandy." She pushed me far enough away to gaze into my eyes. "I like your inner philosopher. One of the things I love about you is how hard you try to get what you feel into words. Especially when we make love."

"So . . . " I sniffed. "Are you saying you love me?"

"I have loved you since you said you believed in my hormones. Well, at least I think so. I mean . . . " She glanced away, blushing. "I couldn't be in love with you, could I? We were friends, and you were gay and I wasn't, and yet every day I woke up thinking how long it would be until I saw you in the morning. And I thought about inventing another set of hormones so

I could ask you . . . more often . . . " The redness across her cheeks intensified.

She was adorable when she blushed, and she wanted . . . me. Well, hell. She *had* fallen in love with the first dyke she went to bed with. My heart was doing cartwheels.

"But I didn't want to lie, and really, I have to warn you, my hormones are real, but ever since you said you believed in them, they haven't been so bad. Ever since you took care of me, more than once, every time . . . it's not so bad. Not so scary."

"I love it when you want it, however you want it." I covered her damp, kissable mouth with mine and everything inside that had ached got hot with a flood of healing. I broke the kiss after a minute with a little laugh. "I love it when you want *me*, however you want me."

She nodded into another kiss and we stayed there for a long time, exploring our mouths like new lovers, like we'd never get enough. I slowly finished unzipping her jumpsuit, slipping my hand inside to cup her bare crotch.

She laughed, low. "Oh, that feels so good. And I am so wet."

I dipped a finger between her swollen lips. "Yes, you are."

She gasped. "I meant the shower, but yes . . . oh."

"Did you wear this for me? So I could reach in to touch you like this?"

"Yes." Her eyes were half-closed, and in spite of the hot water I could see prickles of telltale goose flesh on her arms. "I didn't think you'd be back, but I wanted you. I slept in your bed last night. I missed you so much."

Touched, I kissed her collarbone, then whispered, "I like it when you dress for me."

"You were wearing those naughty panties. Was that for me?"

"Yes, I wanted you to notice."

"Believe me, I did. I thought you wore them for Celine—"

"Uh-uh. For you."

"I thought the note you left, that you wanted to have Valentine's Days and breakfasts meant you might love me, and then it looked like you were going to be with her, and Barbados could call you away, and—"

"Shh." I circled her clit once to feel her knees quiver. "Let's go to bed."

I think she felt as woozy as I did, certainly there was not a lot of oxygen going to my brain. I couldn't tell what was turning me on more, the fact that she wanted me or that she loved me.

Did it matter, as long as both were true?

She was shy. My lovely Tess, who had never been shy about sex with me, was blushing as I drew her down on the bed. "Don't be nervous," I said softly.

"I'm feeling—you know how you got tired of giving straight women lessons?"

"I never felt that way with you," I assured her.

"I want to . . . tell me if I do it wrong."

She was kissing her way down my chest when I realized what she meant. Trembling, I settled back on the bed. My legs jerked when I felt the light brush of her mouth over my pubic hair.

"Are you okay?"

"Yes." I didn't try to stop an earthy moan. "I really don't think you can do it wrong."

"Okay." She didn't look shy anymore. She looked like she was going to eat me alive which was exactly what I wanted. "I want to do it right. You . . . smell so good."

Her tongue slipped between my lips and I shuddered. I felt her hands, then, parting me, opening me, and her tongue covered my clit with a wave of moist heat. I felt delicious and savored, completely loved. Her mouth seemed to envelop my essence, and the small sound of deep pleasure she made sent a hard contraction into the very center of me.

She loved me and her mouth felt wonderful there. She loved

169

me and I could feel it pouring into me from her lips, her tongue and the fingers she slipped inside me. She loved me and my climax was beyond conscious thought. All I could do was feel. For several minutes after, it was all I wanted to do. The only thought I was capable of allowed me to gasp out, "Hold me."

She sighed into my ear and I could smell me on her face. "Wow." She giggled gleefully, then said again, "Wow."

"That's right," I said weakly. "That covers it. Wow."

"I only went out with Gloria because you were with Celine and I didn't think you cared about me that way, and at least I thought I'd get some . . . experience."

"You don't have to account for yourself to me." I took a deep breath and my head cleared. "Well. Now you do. And vice versa, I promise."

"It was ironic that she didn't let me touch her. I liked what she did, but you were better for me, and . . . the second night she wanted to do something and I couldn't. I realized that I felt more safe with her than I did with guys, but I was safe with you, because you're you. You're not just any dyke to me, you're the dyke I love and trust and want."

I sighed happily. I felt so good it could have been a dream. "What did she want to do?" I suspected, but I wanted to be sure. "You don't have to tell me, but . . . if you want that and I could do it, you know I would."

A little shiver went through her. "She said I was . . . very open. She asked if she could put . . . "

I shifted to my side so she was on her back. Leaning over her I bit gently on her lower lip. "I've wanted to do that since the first night. It seemed like more than I had a right to, to be inside you that way. I wasn't supposed to feel that way about you."

"Please, Brandy. I'm not the least bit hormonal—"

"I know—"

"Please, fill me. Take me. It's what I want."

My heart was pounding loud in my ears. "I won't hurt you."

"I know that."

I scrabbled for the lube in the bedside table. I hadn't foreseen this moment, though I had fantasized about it. Except on a tile floor, you can never have too much lube, I told myself. "This is just to be sure."

She nodded, watching me as she spread her legs.

"You are so beautiful." I was momentarily at a loss for words. "So . . . lovely." I bent to her mons, kissing lower until I was kissing her clit. She cooed, that wonderful coo that meant she really liked that, and let my tongue wander through her folds, tasting her sweetness for several minutes.

After an awkward pause to get the lube open, I slathered my hand and rubbed it slowly over her luscious cunt, getting everything wet and slippery.

"Fuck me, Brandy. Please." Tess was breathing hard, and her taut nipples made my mouth water.

I love this woman, I thought. Loving her and feeling her was like touching heaven. I settled next to her so I could take one nipple into my mouth while I let my slick fingers play between her legs.

"Oh, like that. I've wanted this, to feel you like this, I never thought you would—"

"Shh." I coiled my tongue over and around her nipple until she relaxed slightly. "I want you to feel good, feel all my love."

As always, three fingers went into her easily. She moaned and relaxed and my mouth got dry. She was as open as she had ever been, and I knew she could take my hand, but contemplating something so . . . intimate, that required so much trust on her part, was scaring me.

"Take care of me, please."

How could she be so vulnerable? How could she open up like this? Four fingers deep I could feel the inside of her like

171

liquid fire against my knuckles. Maybe—I mean, I did believe she loved me. I believed she meant it, but letting me do this, wanting it to be *me* who took her this way? Maybe she really loved me. "I will, I will, my love. Relax for me, let me . . . slip inside you. Like that."

I put my head on her abdomen and with a gentle push felt my hand go inside her. It fit and it felt right and she moaned, long and deep.

I moaned, too. The feeling of being captured inside her, of touching all of her and her obviously liking it, felt wonderful and safe and trusting and loving, and when her hips moved and she wanted me to stroke inside, that's what I did. Blinking tears out of my eyes I watched her face as I shifted my hand. "More? Do you need more, faster?"

"Yes." She groaned as she tilted her hips up. "Yes, please don't stop!"

"I won't, darling. I'll never stop. Is this okay? Does this feel good?" I pushed a little deeper, then withdrew just a little. Trembling, I curled my fingers around my thumb and turned my fist so my knuckles brushed her G-spot.

"Yes! More . . . "

I lifted my head, my vision swimming at the sight of my wrist disappearing inside her. A big toy, or my hand, what did it matter when her nails were digging into my shoulders and she was begging me to be her lover, to satisfy her, to take care of her? I moved slowly, deliberately, inside her and listened to the music of her moans and pleas and it felt like we were soaring in a place so rare that I never wanted to leave it.

My voice hoarse with desire and love, I said what I had never said before. "I *love* you, I love doing this to you, and I will be here forever, ready to love you, and I am never going to stop."

She shuddered and I felt her entire cunt contract around my hand. My knuckles made contact with her pelvic bone and I

eased up, trying to draw her climax out of her as gently as pos
sible. There might be other ways, other days, other things, but
tonight, filled with love for her, I wanted my hand to give her
more pleasure than either of us could bear.

"My fist is inside you," I said hoarsely, "and I love you."

She cried out. It was the cry I couldn't get enough of, only
louder and longer and deeper in her chest. Her walls seemed to
flutter against my hand, then she got even tighter. I could feel
the wave of her muscles, feel her pleasure rolling from high
inside, through her G-spot and to the tightly stretched muscles
gripping my wrist. I felt like I'd been given the most amazing
gift, to experience her ecstasy so closely.

"Please, please." She was panting. "Go . . . pull out,
please . . . "

"Yes, yes . . . don't worry." I moved gently, and realized with
a tremor of fear that as her climax waned the lube was thinning.
My hand slipped free of her and she groaned—in pain, I
thought. I moved to take her gently into my arms, but she was
grabbing me, pulling me close.

Her hips bucked against me and with awe I realized she was
still coming. I held her tight and close and thrilled to the wild
rolling of her body. I'd made her feel that, by loving her, and I
felt like a supreme being, a creature of pure love.

She gave one long, last gasp before she went limp.

For a minute breathing was all either of us did, then she let
out a helpless laugh. "I don't care what you do to me. If it all
feels that good, you won't be able to get rid of me."

"I love you, Tess. That was more than I ever thought I'd
feel."

She made a little noise as her eyelashes drifted down to meet
her cheeks. One little noise of pleasure and disbelief, then her
breathing steadied and I felt sleep spread through her body.

I laughed to myself as my eyes began to droop as well. That

moment, holding her trusting body in my arms, feeling her relax completely against me, was as pleasurable to me as everything we had just done together.

Falling asleep, with the woman I love in my arms, seemed like a good first step on the road to forever.

I rolled over in bed, blinking in the early morning sunlight. Blonde hair was spread on the pillow next to me, and my motion had gently dislodged her hand from my hip.

I memorized the curves of her face in the fresh light of the new morning. She was smiling slightly. I hoped the good dreams she was having included me. I knew that mine all had included her, and now I wanted to remember my dreams, always.

I touched her hair and inhaled her scent. Nothing could be more sublime than waking up to find her there. It was all wonderful—falling asleep, waking up, touching her, loving her, giving myself to her. The idea that I would get to have these feelings all the time was still so unbelievable that part of me wanted to deny how good it was.

I wasn't going to do that, though. Love was real. Forever isn't a destination, it's a journey.

After another long, satisfying look, I got up to make breakfast.

About the Author

Nice girls do. Nearly halfway through the decade of her forties, that's Karin Kallmaker's new motto. Nice girls do. Fill in the implied blank any way you want.

Karin's first crush on a woman was the local librarian. Just remembering the pencil through the loose, attractive bun makes her warm. Maybe it was the librarian's influence, but for whatever reason, at the age of 16 Karin fell into the arms of her first and only sweetheart.

There's a certain symmetry to the fact that ten years later, after seeing the film *Desert Hearts*, her sweetheart descended on the Berkeley Public Library to find some of "those" books. The books found there were the encouragement Karin needed to forget the so-called "mainstream" and spin her first romance for lesbians. That manuscript became her first novel, *In Every Port. Maybe Next Time* won the 2003 Lambda Literary Award for Best Romance.

The happily ever after couple now lives in the San Francisco Bay area, and became Mom and Moogie to Kelson in 1995 and Eleanor in 1997. They celebrated their twenty-seventh anniversary in 2004.

All of Karin's work can now be found at Bella Books. Details and background about her novels, and her other pen name, Laura Adams, can be found at kallmaker.com.

Publications from
BELLA BOOKS, INC.
The best in contemporary lesbian fiction

P.O. Box 10543, Tallahassee, FL 32302
Phone: 800-729-4992
www.bellabooks.com

TREASURED PAST by Linda Hill. 189 pp. A shared passion for antiques leads to love.
ISBN 1-59493-003-1 $12.95

SIERRA CITY by Gerri Hill. 284 pp. Chris and Jesse cannot deny their growing attraction . . .
ISBN 1-931513-98-8 $12.95

ALL THE WRONG PLACES by Karin Kallmaker. 174 pp. Sex and the single girl—Brandy is looking for love and usually she finds it. Karin Kallmaker's first *After Dark* erotic novel.
ISBN 1-931513-76-7 $12.95

WHEN THE CORPSE LIES A Motor City Thriller by Therese Szymanski. 328 pp. Butch bad-girl Brett Higgins is used to waking up next to beautiful women she hardly knows. Problem is, this one's dead.
ISBN 1-931513-74-0 $12.95

GUARDED HEARTS by Hannah Rickard. 240 pp. Someone's reminding Alyssa about her secret past, and then she becomes the suspect in a series of burglaries.
ISBN 1-931513-99-6 $12.95

ONCE MORE WITH FEELING by Peggy J. Herring. 184 pp. Lighthearted, loving, romantic adventure.
ISBN 1-931513-60-0 $12.95

TANGLED AND DARK A Brenda Strange Mystery by Patty G. Henderson. 240 pp. When investigating a local death, Brenda finds two possible killers—one diagnosed with Multiple Personality Disorder.
ISBN 1-931513-75-9 $12.95

WHITE LACE AND PROMISES by Peggy J. Herring. 240 pp. Maxine and Betina realize sex may not be the most important thing in their lives.
ISBN 1-931513-73-2 $12.95

UNFORGETTABLE by Karin Kallmaker. 288 pp. Can Rett find love with the cheerleader who broke her heart so many years ago?
ISBN 1-931513-63-5 $12.95

HIGHER GROUND by Saxon Bennett. 280 pp. A delightfully complex reflection of the successful, high society lives of a small group of women.
ISBN 1-931513-69-4 $12.95

LAST CALL A Detective Franco Mystery by Baxter Clare. 240 pp. Frank overlooks all else to try to solve a cold case of two murdered children...
ISBN 1-931513-70-8 $12.95

ONCE UPON A DYKE: NEW EXPLOITS OF FAIRY-TALE LESBIANS by Karin Kallmaker, Julia Watts, Barbara Johnson & Therese Szymanski. 320 pp. You've never read fairy tales like these before! From *Bella After Dark*.
ISBN 1-931513-71-6 $14.95

FINEST KIND OF LOVE by Diana Tremain Braund. 224 pp. Can Molly and Carolyn stop clashing long enough to see beyond their differences? ISBN 1-931513-68-6 $12.95

DREAM LOVER by Lyn Denison. 188 pp. A soft, sensuous, romantic fantasy. ISBN 1-931513-96-1 $12.95

NEVER SAY NEVER by Linda Hill. 224 pp. A classic love story… where rules aren't the only things broken. ISBN 1-931513-67-8 $12.95

PAINTED MOON by Karin Kallmaker. 214 pp. Stranded together in a snowbound cabin, Jackie and Leah lives will never be the same. ISBN 1-931513-53-8 $12.95

WIZARD OF ISIS by Jean Stewart. 240 pp. Fifth in the exciting Isis series. ISBN 1-931513-71-4 $12.95

WOMAN IN THE MIRROR by Jackie Calhoun. 216 pp. Josey learns to love again, while her niece is learning to love women for the first time. ISBN 1-931513-78-3 $12.95

SUBSTITUTE FOR LOVE by Karin Kallmaker. 200 pp. When Holly and Reyna meet the combination adds up to pure passion. But what about tomorrow? ISBN 1-931513-62-7 $12.95

GULF BREEZE by Gerri Hill. 288 pp. Could Carly really be the woman Pat has always been searching for? ISBN 1-931513-97-X $12.95

THE TOMSTOWN INCIDENT by Penny Hayes. 184 pp. Caught between two worlds, Eloise must make a decision that will change her life forever. ISBN 1-931513-56-2 $12.95

MAKING UP FOR LOST TIME by Karin Kallmaker. 240 pp. Discover delicious recipes for romance by the undisputed mistress. ISBN 1-931513-61-9 $12.95

THE WAY LIFE SHOULD BE by Diana Tremain Braund. 173 pp. With which woman will Jennifer find the true meaning of love? ISBN 1-931513-66-X $12.95

BACK TO BASICS: A BUTCH/FEMME ANTHOLOGY edited by Therese Szymanski— from Bella After Dark. 324 pp. ISBN 1-931513-35-X $14.95

SURVIVAL OF LOVE by Frankie J. Jones. 236 pp. What will Jody do when she falls in love with her best friend's daughter? ISBN 1-931513-55-4 $12.95

LESSONS IN MURDER by Claire McNab. 184 pp. 1st Detective Inspector Carol Ashton Mystery ISBN 1-931513-65-1 $12.95

DEATH BY DEATH by Claire McNab. 167 pp. 5th Denise Cleever Thriller. ISBN 1-931513-34-1 $12.95

CAUGHT IN THE NET by Jessica Thomas. 188 pp. A wickedly observant story of mystery, danger, and love in Provincetown. ISBN 1-931513-54-6 $12.95

DREAMS FOUND by Lyn Denison. Australian Riley embarks on a journey to meet her birth mother . . . and gains not just a family, but the love of her life. ISBN 1-931513-58-9 $12.95

A MOMENT'S INDISCRETION by Peggy J. Herring. 154 pp. Jackie is torn between her better judgment and the overwhelming attraction she feels for Valerie. ISBN 1-931513-59-7 $12.95

IN EVERY PORT by Karin Kallmaker. 224 pp. Jessica has a woman in every port. Will meeting Cat will change all that? ISBN 1-931513-36-8 $12.95

TOUCHWOOD by Karin Kallmaker. 240 pp. Rayann loves Louisa. Louisa loves Rayann. Can the decades between their ages keep them apart?   ISBN 1-931513-37-6 $12.95

WATERMARK by Karin Kallmaker. 248 pp. Teresa wants a future with a woman whose heart has been frozen by loss. Sequel to *Touchwood*.   ISBN 1-931513-38-4 $12.95

EMBRACE IN MOTION by Karin Kallmaker. 240 pp. Has Sarah found lust or love?
ISBN 1-931513-39-2 $12.95

ONE DEGREE OF SEPARATION by Karin Kallmaker. 232 pp. Sizzling small town romance between Marian, the town librarian, and the new girl from the big city.
ISBN 1-931513-30-9 $12.95

CRY HAVOC A Detective Franco Mystery by Baxter Clare. 240 pp. A dead hustler with a headless rooster in his lap sends Lt. L.A. Franco headfirst against Mother Love.
ISBN 1-931513931-7 $12.95

DISTANT THUNDER by Peggy J. Herring. 294 pp. Bankrobbing drifter Cordy awakens strange new feelings in Leo in this romantic tale set in the Old West.
ISBN 1-931513-28-7 $12.95

COP OUT by Claire McNab. 216 pp. 4th Detective Inspector Carol Ashton Mystery.
ISBN 1-931513-29-5 $12.95

BLOOD LINK by Claire McNab. 159 pp. 15th Detective Inspector Carol Ashton Mystery. Is Carol unwittingly playing into a deadly plan?   ISBN 1-931513-27-9 $12.95

TALK OF THE TOWN by Saxon Bennett. 239 pp. With enough beer, barbecue and B.S., anything is possible!   ISBN 1-931513-18-X $12.95

MAYBE NEXT TIME by Karin Kallmaker. 256 pp. Sabrina has everything she ever wanted—except Jorie.   ISBN 1-931513-26-0 $12.95

WHEN GOOD GIRLS GO BAD: A Motor City Thriller by Therese Szymanski. 230 pp. Brett, Randi, and Allie join forces to stop a serial killer.   ISBN 1-931513-11-2 $12.95

A DAY TOO LONG: A Helen Black Mystery by Pat Welch. 328 pp. This time Helen's fate is in her own hands.   ISBN 1-931513-22-8 $12.95

THE RED LINE OF YARMALD by Diana Rivers. 256 pp. The Hadra's only hope lies in a magical red line . . . climactic sequel to *Clouds of War*.   ISBN 1-931513-23-6 $12.95

OUTSIDE THE FLOCK by Jackie Calhoun. 224 pp. Jo embraces her new love and life.
ISBN 1-931513-13-9 $12.95

LEGACY OF LOVE by Marianne K. Martin. 224 pp. Read the whole Sage Bristo story.
ISBN 1-931513-15-5 $12.95

STREET RULES: A Detective Franco Mystery by Baxter Clare. 304 pp. Gritty, fast-paced mystery with compelling Detective L.A. Franco.   ISBN 1-931513-14-7 $12.95

RECOGNITION FACTOR: 4th Denise Cleever Thriller by Claire McNab. 176 pp. Denise Cleever tracks a notorious terrorist to America.   ISBN 1-931513-24-4 $12.95

NORA AND LIZ by Nancy Garden. 296 pp. Lesbian romance by the author of *Annie on My Mind*.   ISBN 1931513-20-1 $12.95

MIDAS TOUCH by Frankie J. Jones. 208 pp. Sandra had everything but love.
ISBN 1-931513-21-X $12.95